# ICARUS IN REVERSE

## And Other Stories

Dominic O'Sullivan

Shield Crest

© Copyright 2013 Dominic O'Sullivan

All rights reserved

This book shall not, by way of trade or otherwise, be lent, re-sold, hired out, or otherwise circulated without the prior consent of the copyright holder or the publisher in any form of binding or cover other than that in which it is published and without a similar condition including this condition being imposed on the subsequent purchaser. The use of its contents in any other media is also subject to the same conditions.

ISBN   978-1-907629-92-1

MMXIII

Published by
ShieldCrest
Aylesbury, Buckinghamshire, HP22 5RR
England
www.shieldcrest.co.uk

*To Peter and Mary*

*With special thanks to Michael Bardouleau*

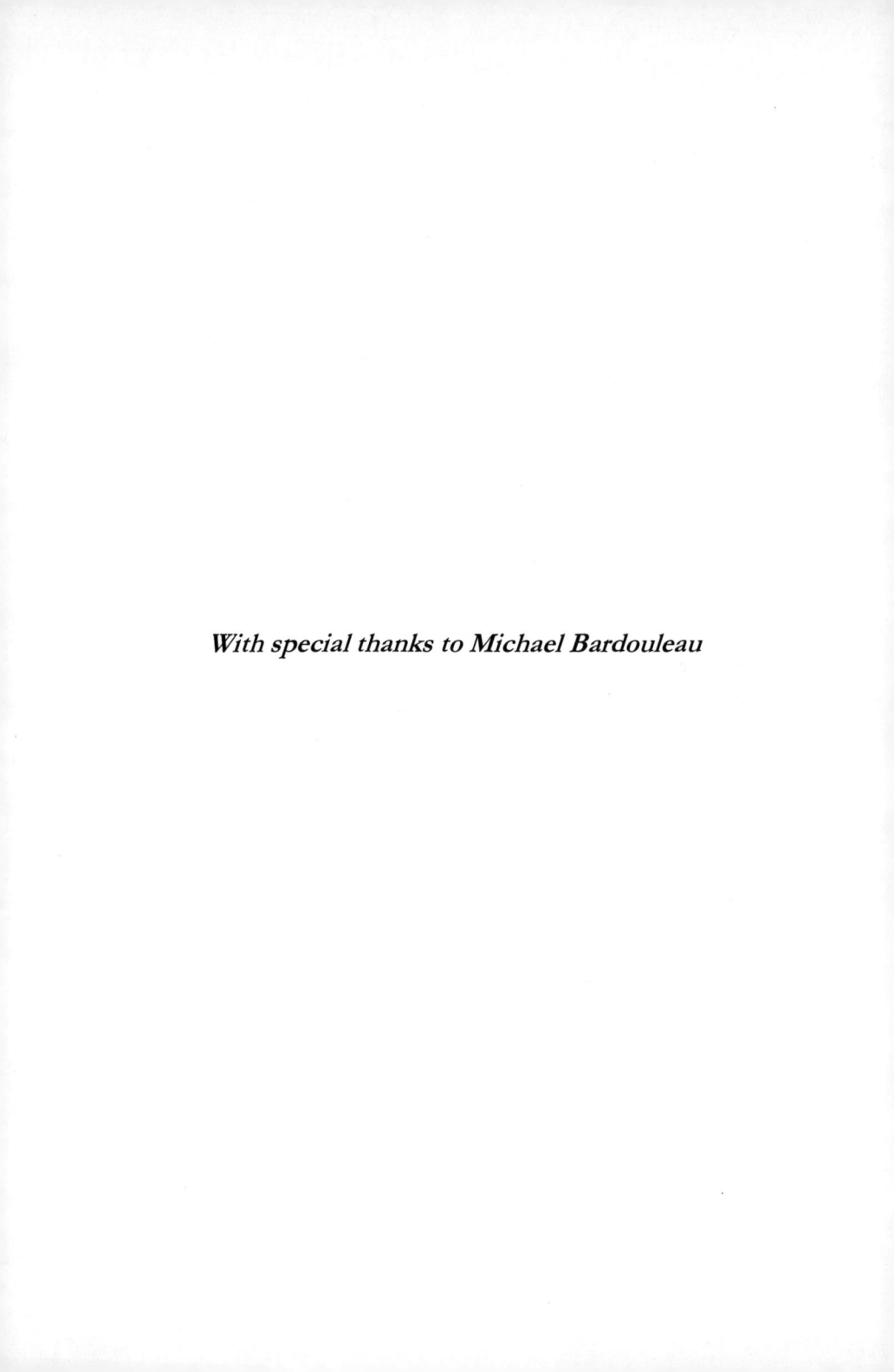

## About the Author

Dominic O'Sullivan was born in North London and grew up in Muswell Hill. He has, however, spent much of his time in East Anglia. He studied German at the University of East Anglia under the guidance of his tutor Dr W.G. 'Max' Sebald.

In 2009 he published his first collection of short stories 'Swifts' of which the title story was performed as a play in the Chocolate Factory, North London.

In this collection both 'New Wave' and 'A Dash of Soda' were performed at the ADC Theatre in Cambridge in May 2013 as part of a season of monologues and dialogues

# Contents

| | |
|---|---|
| Icarus in Reverse | 1 |
| Awaybreak | 7 |
| The Pond | 14 |
| The Balcony | 21 |
| Cairina Moschata | 27 |
| A Variety of Accents | 38 |
| The Preparation | 46 |
| Codpiece | 50 |
| Widdershins | 58 |
| Birdsong | 61 |
| New Wave | 65 |
| Ultimate Predictions | 67 |
| The Clarity of Dialogue | 77 |
| A Dash of Soda | 88 |
| Holy Orders | 95 |
| Without Eaves | 102 |
| Kop Kun Krap | 107 |
| Nocturne | 114 |
| In Passing | 116 |
| Listening | 120 |
| The Uncertainties of Verbs | 126 |

# Icarus in Reverse

I think, in the circumstances, I had no other course of action. I mean, necessity called for a period of absentia after that fateful morning.

I still see myself at my desk, gathering up the documents, engravings, pens, papers, things that have adorned and sprawled across the vast expanse of wood. For a moment I placed my hand across its smooth surface. It has been a faithful companion to me in my somewhat mediocre existence – a calming, thoughtful presence rendered all the more so by its solidity, its intrinsic immobility.

If only it had detained me on that dreadful day, kept me occupied, though in truth nothing could really have explained my absence! We were all requested, nay commanded, to be in attendance of our gracious, sovereign lady. She had been away for some little while at the house in Hatfield. As a relatively new edifice it still possesses a certain solemnity, a grace, and when you step into its light and airy corridors, so I'm told, an inherent warmth and welcome is projected.

I see her riding through the surrounding countryside, passing the sloping fields with all the lanes ablaze in shades of hawthorn. It is of marked contrast to *my* sorry departure which I took upon myself the very next day. Alone, I made my way through the thoroughfares of Kent towards the coast. I stopped at various places en route, reaching my destination some four days later. A sea mist lurked spitefully there and I discovered I would have to wait two more days for a departure.

In my mind's eye I saw my vacated chamber, bereft now of its incumbent, with sunlight filtering slowly into the middle of the room, catching the darkened panels between the tapestries.

I could hear the silence, feel it almost!

As I was saying we were all duly summoned to meet our gracious lady. On a raised plinth she sat while we stood and in turn came to make our bows, our obeisance. Her pale face seemed all the paler under her flame-coloured hair, which Megan in the kitchen nastily said was a wig. If you ask me, Megan is of the 'old' persuasion and is no doubt a follower of our dear lady's late half-sister. These are awkward times, you see, made harder by the 'fluctuations', progressions and defections, reversals and... There is some anxiety too as to whether the Scottish queen will take over the reins and then it'll be all change again. The Lord in Heaven must be quite confused at all the varying rituals being offered to Him – though I expect perhaps it's all the same; a kind of buzzing inside the ear. Adulation is but adulation, praise is merely praise.

I was about fourteenth in the line of assembled homage makers with Dewsbury immediately behind me. If you ask me he is a shifty little devil, mealy-mouthed and I'm sure not greatly esteemed by our gracious lady. After Appleton had made his bow, kissing the fingers of our fair lady's hand, it was now my turn.

"How now, my lord?" she enquired.

I bent towards her, a leaning tree in a gusty breeze. I decided I would bend yet further to show that knave Dewsbury the affection in which I was likely to be held. I inclined all the more and as I did so, I felt a strange rippling sensation pass within my stomach. It seemed to subside swiftly enough and then, just as I was about to intone the

## Icarus In Reverse

words 'My gracious Lady', I thought I could hear a slight soprano buzzing within the room. It continued a moment in modulation and as I leaned forward a little further in appropriate devotion it suddenly deepened. To my profoundest horror I could feel vigorous vibrations and rumblings within my nether regions and realised I was the victim of a full-blown fart!

I could sense the assembly gazing on aghast. There was the sound of fidgeting footsteps behind – no doubt that odious Dewsbury caught in full blast. My gracious lady's smile retracted a little, perhaps in surprise at my own forwardness. I felt myself reddening, turning from sombre carrot to hawthorn and beetroot, retrieving my balance awkwardly after the sabotage of this hideous, unwanted emission. I took my place alongside the others in the wings and wished that one of the nearby curtains would obscure me, carry me off...

Dewsbury bowed his obsequious bow and the lady received him with enquiry and familiar condescension. In fact, she had spoken more to him than to me, which was perhaps a sign of her own displeasure. If a whale had drifted past the assembled court I would willingly have jumped into its cavernous jaws and been gone in a trice forever!

Oh, the shame of it! A hiccup of the nether regions! An eructation before our gracious Sovereign! An unfortunate case of Icarus in reverse! Instead of flying above the clouds I had set myself too low...

I averted eyes in corridors, gazed into the neutral distance, which in itself was not much comfort. It would not be long before word would spread – I would be victim of the smug smirks from serving wenches – my name, my very being, my reputation – and there would be the sly, supercilious, self-satisfied smile of Daniel Dewsbury.

I resolved to pack and leave the very next day. The rest you know, of course.

I took up employment some months later in the north of France. They'd sent some little prince over to woo our lady and relationships were somewhat cordiale at the time. I'm spelling it with an 'e' you'll notice. It seems much more French and cultured.

The Duke or Duc was greatly impressed that I had attended the Court presided over by our Sovereign lady. He was always asking questions such as 'What colour stockings does she wear?' or 'What does she have for breakfast?' How should I know and be party to such things? 'Many and various' was the answer I often essayed and it seemed to suffice.

As for my duties, when I was not answering questions of a wildly impertinent nature, I was obliged to oversee the running of the house – its internal workings, its finances and potential. I was given the most magnificent chamber to work in, its view looking out onto a deer park whose inhabitants were constantly rutting and procreating. There was a noble crystal chandelier above and three large windows which opened out onto a garden.

And yet I missed certain things. My old desk for one, with its calming, soothing and sympathetic surface. There was Robin the stable-boy who invariably greeted me with a saucy wink and whose meaning I had yet to fathom. Then there was the Lady Wenderley whose cakes were a trial for any tooth; and there was plenteous ale flowing at the Frog and Nightgown, a curious juxtaposition for a liquor house. All these things combined and exerted the pull and pain of absence.

After five years of contemplating the endlessly rutting deer I resolved to return home. I was embraced by the Duc and more fervently by his wife, who muttered something incomprehensible about English boys.

Then I found myself gazing at Albion's impending cliffs in trepidation, snow-white like the colour of my stomach. I stepped off the barque switching immediately to my native

## Icarus In Reverse

tongue. It was odd to hear myself speaking it, spiced as it was with a faint Gallic twang.

I made my way back through the lanes of Kent, where the umbellifers, if anything, had grown much taller. On reaching my destination I experienced yet more anxiety but immediately I was spotted by the Lady Wenderley and Robin. They supplied me with rock cakes and a wink.

I noticed that in my absence their 'langue de corps' had grown a little more intimate.

"But you are speaking French!" said the Lady Wenderley, offering me another rock cake.

"Pardon," I replied, my lips full of currants.

"Also French," said the Lady Wenderley dismissively and Robin sniggered.

I was shown back to Court. There was a vacancy, Lord Puddleborough having been taken by the gout. I returned to my old office with the same tapestries and desk. I flung open the windows to the welcome smell of cow dung. No antlers ambled by.

I felt I had undergone a period of expiation, of necessary exile after the... the... I could scarcely remember it myself or was it that the pain had erased the memory?

It was Friday and we were all assembled before the Queen. She looked radiant and pale and golden. I was the next in line, for in the passage of time we now shuffled a little slower.

My throat was temporarily dry, parched, a symptom no doubt of Lady Wenderley's peculiar confections.

"You are most welcome, sir," quod the gracious lady, extending an arm in my direction.

I digested the remains of the rock cake and smiled at her comely radiance.

"We had quite forgot the fart," she continued.

I hesitated as I swayed before her. 'Most gracious lady' were the words I had formulated within, yet somehow her greeting had taken me by surprise. I felt a little uncertain, disrupted.

I'm not entirely sure but perhaps it was the confidence gained from those years abroad; the freedom of being a foreigner in a place where language has not the same ties nor snares. A riposte was forming and, like the emission of old, the one that had necessitated my departure, it took me a little by surprise. I raised myself up an inch or so.

"It is a sad arsehole that never rejoices, madam!"

There was a shrill hush in the assembled court, a moment where sound and movement dies, and like a happy winged bird plummets suddenly to earth. Had I indeed done it again? Had history repeated itself?

I saw the lanes of Kent, the frothy umbellifers, the hugely listing ferry. I saw the Duke and Duchess and myself speaking French again. She did, however, make a very good cake.

The pause lasted a while longer but it was my lady who finally broke it.

"Indeed, sir. And yours perhaps is merrier than most. Arise, my liege."

I did and without mishap.

All was well. The winged bird was airborne again – a sort of gull gazing upon the sands of time. No longer was I to witness the croaking, rutting deer.

"My gracious lady," I replied gratefully.

To which she smiled and…did my eyes deceive me but was there the vaguest semblance of a wink?

# Awaybreak

"Three o'clock," repeated Elsie as she placed the phone down. "That's fine, then."
She put the kettle on and went into the garden. It felt surprisingly sunny. Beyond the fence, Mrs. Lampitt was hanging out the washing.

"Good drying weather," said Elsie.

"Yes," said Mrs. Lampitt. "Yes."

She didn't say much. It was Elsie who had to make all the conversation. "They're coming at three o'clock," she continued.

"What's that for?" asked Nora Lampitt.

"Carer's assessment," Elsie replied. "They come every six months."

"Oh," said Nora. "You'll have some visitors, then?"

"I think it's just to see I'm still here. That I'm not getting money under false pretences." She laughed.

"I see," said Nora. She had finished hanging out the washing and headed back inside.

People were funny, Elsie thought. I mean, there's not much wrong with Nora, but she never asks after Arnie. Never asks. Perhaps she thinks I'm living here on my own and that shape at the window, that slouched figure is a ghost.

A blackbird was hopping across the lawn, as if on springs. It was still damp from the overnight rain. The garden had been lovely once, when he looked after it. Wallflowers – she loved the smell – and nasturtiums creeping under the window. Daffodils, too. And those tall blue flowers with spikes. She could never remember their name.

She sat with him a while, thinking back to when he was out in the garden. She held his hand a moment.

"They're coming at three, Arnie," she said. He didn't react. "They'll probably want to say hello. See how you're doing, so don't get worried if…" She looked at his shock of dishevelled hair. It had been long and dark once. "We'd better smarten you up."

She reached for the grey comb on the nearby table. He gazed beyond Elsie and out towards the window. Could he see the sun outside, she wondered? She'd love to be able to push him out into the garden so that he could feel the warmth on his face. Just for a moment. But they'd said better not, what with the risk of infections and all that.

"It's a lovely day, Arnie," she said, squeezing his hand once again.

It was ten past three when she came. A new one. Hadn't seen her before. A silvery Mercedes slid past the front door. For what seemed an age she remained inside the car, finally to emerge with a briefcase and folder.

Elsie was at the door.

"Mrs. Blackwell." Her visitor offered a limp hand. "I'm Elizabeth Norrington."

"Yes," Elsie replied. "We spoke on the phone."

"We did."

Norrington. She'd heard that name before, she thought. It was a town somewhere.

Elsie released the hand. She wasn't keen on shaking hands with women. It was nearly always a soft, flimsy handshake. She liked a large firm hand, one that you could get lost in. Yes, it was much better shaking hands with men, she decided.

"Would you like a cup of tea?"

"No, thank you," said Elizabeth.

"Biscuit, maybe?"

The woman laughed. "I'll get terribly fat."

Elsie wondered how this was possible, seeing as she was paper thin. Nobody seemed to drink anything nowadays; never when they came. Perhaps they thought the water was contaminated in this part of town or she'd poison the tea. As if!

"And how is Arthur doing?"

"It's Arnie," Elsie corrected her.

"I'm so sorry. Arnie. As you can imagine, we have quite a lot of clients."

Clients! It made her sound like a tart! Elsie poured herself a cup of tea. It tasted good in company.

"And how is Arnie doing?"

"Much the same."

"Can he say anything? Do you know if he's comfortable?"

She shook her head. "He's not uncomfortable."

"And do family and friends pop in?"

"We manage," Elsie said.

The last but one woman had wanted to know the names of those who dropped by. Was putting together some sort of profile. On Arnie!

"I told her it was none of her business," she'd said to Mrs. Lampitt later in the day.

"Quite right," agreed Mrs. Lampitt. She felt to see if the washing was dry.

"Can I see the medication?" Mrs. Norrington asked.

Elsie passed the folder to her. "The pills and things is over there."

"Right, fine."

Elsie looked at her visitor's smart grey jacket and matching dress. It made her look like an administrator dressed for a conference, not at all like the usual ones from the Council. She must have a bob or two, she thought. That car!

The visitor was meticulously writing down all the names of the medication. It took a while.

"I give 'em names," Elsie said. "Them pink ones there are Bill. The ones with the hundreds and thousands in, Fred."

"I hope you don't mix them up," the visitor said.

"No. That's why I do it. All those pill names sound the same, so I write on the list two Bills, three Freds, and that little tiny one, I call Jasper. Arnie doesn't like that one."

"Does he say so?"

"I can tell."

"I still think you should learn their proper names. What if you have to give the information over the phone to someone?"

"Well, if it's the doctor, they'd know already. I find the milkman doesn't usually ask."

"The milkman?" Mrs. Norrington failed to see the connection or relevance.

Yes, thought Elsie. She's a bit serious, this one. You couldn't have a laugh with her, unlike that Irish girl who came before.

"What's happened to Fiona?" she asked, suddenly remembering her name.

"Fiona?"

"The last one."

"What was her second name?"

"Oh, I can't remember that."

"We've had some restructuring in our department."

"Pity," said Elsie, pointedly. "I liked her."

Restructuring! Sounded more like painters and decorators!

"I was wondering about my break."

"A break?"

"Yes. Last time they said I could have one."

"You mean in the evening?"

"No. A proper break. Like a weekend or something. They give you money to go away somewhere. The first girl said I could have it, but the second one didn't seem to know. Couldn't find anything about it. I keep seeing different people, you see. Fiona said I was definitely entitled to it and she was going to look into it."

" As far as I'm aware, she's no longer in the department. I'll need to check the paperwork."

"Having a baby, is she?"

"I wouldn't know."

"Lovely girl. She'd make somebody a good wife. Good at chatting, she was. We used to have a laugh. Her auntie got locked in the lavatory."

Mrs. Norrington had finished writing.

"Is he eating properly? Regular meals?"

"He eats when he wants to."

"And you do the cooking? The carers who come in the morning don't do any…?"

"No, I do it."

"Right."

There was a silence. She was looking at something in her folder. Suddenly she got up.

"Could I see Mr. Blackwell now?"

Elsie smiled. It seemed funny Arnie being referred to as Mr. Blackwell. It made him sound like someone else; somebody quite important. The bank manager, possibly.

"He's in the back room," she said.

They both entered. Arnie sat there with his back to them, staring out of the window.

"Someone to see you, love."

She noticed that Mrs. Norrington stood over him and didn't sit down next to him as Fiona did. Fiona would always take his hand, and at one time, Elsie thought, she'd even got a flicker of a smile out of him. Always liked a pretty girl did Arnie.

"How are you keeping, Mr. Blackwell?" She bent down towards him.

Arnie had seen a bird in the garden, Elsie thought. He had that look. Yes. Very possibly as Arnie's drifting gaze was following its flight.

Mrs. Norrington stayed for a minute or two looking at him.

"I think perhaps we should go in the other room," Elsie suggested. "He doesn't like being talked about."

"Does he say that?"

"No, but I can tell. I know."

They sat back down again in the other room while Mrs. Norrington finished her paperwork.

"My sister Jessie from Huddersfield says she'd come down and look after him if I had a break. She's quite willing to."

"Right, I need you to sign this."

"What's it say?"

"That you're happy with the care package."

Elsie reached for her glasses. "It's a package now, is it?" She thought for a moment. "What does that mean?"

"The programme of support and counselling. The agreement between Service Provider and Service User."

"I see. Yes. Well, I suppose I am."

She signed in the box that the finger guided her to.

"Yes, you see, I thought I'd go up to Norfolk. Have a run by the sea. There's still a train that goes up there."

"As I said, I'll look into it for you."

"That'd be nice." There was a pause. "How long would it be?"

"I couldn't really say. I have to put it to my Line Manager for approval."

"Only the winter's coming soon and Jessie doesn't like travelling in the winter. It's quite a way for her."

Mrs. Norrington got up. She was making towards the front door. She stretched out her hand again, which Elsie took. It seemed to have grown even smaller.

*Icarus In Reverse*

"It's been nice meeting you," she said.

"Yes," said Elsie.

She took something out of her pocket and pointed it towards the car. There was a click from within and the front lights came on.

Elsie saw her put the briefcase and folder inside on the back seat. In a few moments, she was driving off down the lane, wheel marks on the grass, and gone. She didn't look back to return Elsie's wave.

"Somewhere by the sea," Elsie said.

# The Pond

I suppose you could say I had a hand in things. Perhaps a bit more than that, but not with the first. Definitely not the first. The poor old sod was no more than a living corpse shuffling from one space to the next. It was a real triumph of will to mount the podium, for instance. Those few final steps towards the glorious May Day Parade.

And from there, in the company of his grey-suited 'cousins', he would impart the gentlest of waves to the colonnades, the tanks that flowed effortlessly past in their awe-inspiring display of might. Then afterwards came the collected speeches to the Assembly. So often interminable.

It was during one that I noticed he'd had a minor accident, a slight urinary release, and I realised that things were going to change.

They used to joke about his bushy eyebrows, saying they were the aftermath of you know who's moustache. Of course he did very little to reverse 'those practices'. In the ensuing years of 'stagnation' as they became known as – after the interlude of the bald teddy bear – almost nothing changed. The same persuasive techniques, malpractices, and the abuse of hospitals.

My auntie's neighbour found himself carted off to one in his pyjamas one morning for speaking out of turn. We were subsequently careful thereafter to sever all links. Auntie quickly moved. I was able to arrange a transfer for her so that the trail from auntie to neighbour and inevitably me was appropriately removed. It was like taking up railway tracks; extracting sleepers so that it became a branch line to nowhere. I was safe, and with me my ultimate responsibility.

In the latter days, I found him sitting there, immobile in his chair like some lost Pharaoh. On hearing me come into the room, he would slowly incline his head like some slumbering lizard, very gently as if trying to bring me within his focus. And then the head would turn back affording a profile of a heavy eyebrow as he meandered off into a contemplation of nothingness. Towards the end there would almost be no movement at all and he would continue staring straight ahead, gazing out through the large windows.

One afternoon I was arranging the books on the bookshelf – it always looked good when we had visitors so I was constantly rearranging, each lifted book jacket an affirmation of my worth, my usefulness, my calming domestic presence, because you couldn't trust some of those visitors or what they were likely to say – and he said "Where am I?"

"At home, sir," I replied, briefly refraining from my gentle dusting.

"And where's that?" he asked.

"Home!"

Astonished I repeated the name of the address, the region.

"And where's that?" he continued.

I stated the obvious, the name of our beloved country, our great city.

"I see," he said. "And who runs it?"

I thought he was joking, perhaps leading up to a veiled critique of those useless hangers-on, those unpleasant machinators and manipulators, those parasitical Party apparatchiks.

"*You* do, sir," I replied.

He gazed at me very intently, questioningly, as if I were humouring him.

"Since when?" he enquired.

I had to think for a moment for it felt like he'd been around forever. I had to be perfectly precise with the dates. It could, after all, be a trap and I had to be meticulous in the glorious chronology.

Just as I was assembling an impressive and speedily prepared listing of dates, there was an enormous gurgling sound to my left. I glanced across and Our Great Leader had suddenly fallen asleep. I was therefore unable to deliver the collection of meaningful dates with the appropriate interspersed eulogies. I'm still not sure if he knew who he was when he went to sleep that chilly night and failed to wake up the following morning.

It took a while to impart the news. We had to be *so* careful. It was as if we had all been victim to some paralysis or infection and we had to wait some time for the all clear.

Then came the shock! The mourning. The sense of unreality as if everybody was dreaming. Tributes came from expected and less predictable sources. They attested to greatness, to wisdom, to flexibility, to the 'ongoing commitment to peace'. Of course they omitted to mention the 'years of stagnation' during which a coat of thick green slime had started to slither across the pond.

The successor, the pale man who came afterwards, appeared more energetic. It would have been hard not to have been! A tortoise is after all quicker than a sloth. He had a keen eye for detail, was a meticulous observer, which was appropriate, I suppose, for a former Head of Secret Police.

And here I pause to pay tribute to that 'lifeblood', the protectors of our system, those silent guardian angels, and to those whom we hold so dear.

He was a lover of flowers, unexpectedly – the new man. Bright yellows adorned the office; an astonishing outburst of colour after the lengthy years of grey. He carried on in the same mould, of course, the same hostile rhetoric, but even *he*

## Icarus In Reverse

gazed down at the pond of congealed slime and expressed a mild concern for change.

It didn't happen, naturally. Merely a contemplation, but the flowers were nice. I had to inspect them daily because one time various bugs were found within. I'm referring to the insect kind. Little black dots and whirly things that trundled around anti-clockwise all day. And as they did so, they became encrusted in pollen from the long straggly stamens. An intoxication of fertility perhaps. He had a morbid fear of spiders. One crossed the drawing room carpet one day and from nowhere came this piercing scream. I attended to the miscreant with its excess of legs.

"It's only a spider, sir," I confirmed.

He would not look at me until I had removed the thing.

"Where do they come from?" he asked afterwards.

I gazed at him, puzzled. "Surely they are everywhere, sir," I replied.

"Everywhere? In the building?"

"Why yes, sir. I assure you, it's quite normal."

"Normal? But how do they get in?"

I thought of their favourite route, the bathrooms, the subterranean world of plugs and washbasins, pipes.

"Shall I see to it, sir, that they do not bother you in future?"

I noticed a drop of sweat on those pale and sallow cheeks. He nodded quickly, gazing back towards the cheery daffs.

"Not the flowers?" he asked.

"Oh no, sir. Not the flowers."

But from then on I had to check them meticulously every hour as if they were guilty of harbouring miscreants.

"The flowers," he would say. There was no need to finish the sentence. I would attend immediately.

And then, of course, they gradually stopped coming. Disappeared altogether. Striped cheerfulness that caught the morning sun. Exiled. We were back to the sombre shades of grey.

Then one day, when I was tidying up the drawing room, dusting the heavy polished oak tables at which the favoured few would sit and converse, I heard a solitary scream.

It appeared to come from the first floor bathroom so I called out in my dutiful concerned voice. There was no reply. I came up the stairs and called again. Still no answer. I pushed open the door, glad that sir had not chosen to slide the bolt. His balding head was blocking easy access so I squeezed past to witness the flimsy dressing gown that partly concealed the nether regions of our Esteemed Leader.

Scurrying back to the safety of the pot plant I had somehow failed to remove was an innocent arachnid scaling its homespun sticky thread. It was beetling away, if you'll pardon the pun, like a silent assassin seeking the safety of a crowd.

They took less time than with the previous incumbent to announce the tragic news. Even the West was in shock. He hadn't lasted very long, but all in all there was no conjecture, no suspicion unlike the various intrigues that were surrounding the unfortunate thirty three day Pope.

He was a reformer, I suppose. Going to make changes, clear up the debris in the years of...stagnation possibly. It's good, you see, for us to apply a little of our own reciprocal logic. But it was strange nonetheless.

The next one – I'm going back to us now – was even older. A peculiar choice, I thought, but then I suppose everyone was caught on the hop. I was a little concerned that they were going to ask me to pack my suitcase but luckily there was no mention of it at the present time.

The new man disliked visitors on the whole and although he wouldn't admit it, they caused him a bit of strain. I noticed his breathing becoming heavier, his hands giving way to a slight tremor. The first speech he delivered on ascending the throne – I'm sorry about that – included some sabre-rattling towards the West. It's always good to get the nation behind you, point fingers at the fiends lurking beyond the mist.

I applauded him on it when the visitors had gone. He merely asked for a dry sherry.

"Are we celebrating, sir?" I asked.

"*I* am," he replied.

I felt mildly affronted. There was an element of rebuff in this. Even the first Master, comatose and corpse-like that he was, would have offered and motioned to me to fetch a glass. But this one sat back and simply savoured the drink. As his overlarge head rested against the tastefully embroidered antimacassar, which had been a present from a grateful auntie, he suddenly asked "What's that noise?"

"Noise, sir?"

"Yes, noise."

"I hear no noise."

"Listen."

He put down the glass on the silver trolley. I listened.

"There's nothing, sir."

"There *is*."

"Maybe just the wind in the chimneys."

"I'll give you wind in the chimneys!"

And then I listened. Really listened. Taking in all the sounds in that heavily carpeted room.

"Might it be the clock, sir?"

"Clock?" He looked alarmed. "Is there a clock?"

"It's useful, sir."

"Take it away!" he shouted. "If there's one thing I can't bear it's a clock ticking in a silent room!"

I was about to say how much the previous Party Secretary had liked that clock or to suggest that we could make more noise to mask it when suddenly I saw a train ticket to Siberia begin to float before my eyes.

"And even worse in a bedroom!" he added.

I dutifully removed the clock.

"Much better," he said, basking now in the total silence of the airless and daffodil-free room.

"Will that be all?" I asked.

He nodded.

Some weeks later he quietly expired in the night. I waited a little while before I made the necessary call; tiptoed softly round the building.

But before I did so, I removed from the table opposite beside the king-sized bed a small and diminutive object. In my haste to dust the flat the previous morning it had inadvertently travelled from the kitchen cupboard and into the Master's boudoir. It never came under suspicion.

Three in a row, I thought, smiling now at the immensely younger successor, who had a port-wine mark on his head.

For now it seemed there really was someone to drain away the pond.

Of course I kept my silence and told no one.

*Icarus In Reverse*

# The Balcony

Ellen glanced over at the clock that was ticking loudly by the trolley. Sometimes she noticed it, sometimes she didn't. There were days when there was nothing to be heard at all, as if a soft fleecy blanket had lined the whole room and taken up every vibration, every sound. But today she heard it and gazed at it, this small diminutive clock that ticked away every second but whose wake-up call lay permanently stranded at half past six.

Twenty to. Twenty to, it was now. And in a few minutes they would be here. One o'clock. The one o'clock lunch visit. This signified no problems, held no terrors in itself, but the four o'clock today, well that was going to be different.

She could hear footsteps on the stairs, a light being switched on. There was no need, Ellen thought. You could see perfectly well.

"Hello!" called a voice.

Megan was in the doorway, her big bustling frame looking for a tray that needed to go downstairs.

"Hello, dear," said Ellen.

"I can't find it," Megan complained.

"Can't find what, dear?"

"The little tray."

Megan sighed audibly.

"I don't think I had one this morning. I managed okay, though."

Megan was pursing her lips in irritation. Some of these younger carers were a bit slapdash, a bit carefree. They should have looked in the book. It was what it was there for, all clearly there. And if they'd done so, they would have seen how it was meant to be.

"No harm done, I suppose."

The gently vibrating buttocks indicated displeasure as Megan tidied up a few magazines.

"What if you'd spilt your tea?" she asked. "What then?"

"But I didn't."

"But if you had?"

"I'd tell myself to be more careful in future."

"But that's not the point, dear!"

Megan always highlighted the word 'dear' when she was annoyed. Ellen glanced away to the large lime tree beyond the window. It was on the point of shedding its leaves. The woman was at her side now.

"I'm not cross with you," she soothed.

"No, I know you're not," Ellen replied.

"It's just sometimes they forget."

"We all forget."

"But they should know the form."

"Yes," said Ellen.

It didn't matter now. She smiled at Megan.

"I don't think you're taking this seriously, dear," Megan mock-chided.

"Oh, but I am, dear."

There was a sudden noise from outside.

"Is that Melissa?"

"No, love. It's that fat grey and black tabby. It just fell off the fence."

"Ah yes. The neighbour's garden, I expect. The freedom of the outdoors."

Megan was clearing away some magazines.

## Icarus In Reverse

"I used to tell them," Ellen continued. "You're feeding it far too much. It'll soon be the size of a small puma."

Megan saw the cat recuperate, stretch its whole body and continue to saunter regally along the path. If only we could fall like that, she thought. Borrow some of those nine lives. She saw the flicking tail disappear among the rose bushes.

"Will you be back at four?" Ellen asked her.

"No, love," said Megan. "It's the other carers. You know the other company."

Oh, of course. The other company.

"They're going to do a risk something," said Ellen.

"A risk assessment," Megan replied.

"See if I need..."

"You show them," Megan encouraged.

"There's that dreadful woman with the clipboard. I can never understand her. She talks like a train. Rattles away. Always making notes. Keeps asking me how I feel."

"And what do you say?" Megan asked.

"Same as when you last asked me three minutes ago. Or that I was fine until some stupid busybody came along and started asking foolish questions."

"No," said Megan emphatically. "It's not the way. You have to humour them. Pander to them a little."

Ellen nodded. "Never underestimate the power of a clerk."

"Precisely!"

"But I feel like some kind of performing seal having to stand up and do those things. And when she's here I always walk much worse. I can see her looking at me, staring at me above that ghastly clipboard."

"I'm sure it won't be too bad." Megan was squeezing Ellen's hand gently. "I'll be rooting for you."

"I'm glad," said Ellen, "That you'll be rooting..."

The afternoon was full of rain. Grey inflatable clouds which puffed beyond the window sending squally bursts of rain against the panes of glass. For a moment she thought about the window cleaner, of how she used to pay him and how he usually wanted a cup of tea. He used to come at inconvenient times when the brewing up of a tea or coffee would prove irksome. His boy was much nicer, though. Michael. Quite quiet really. Almost reticent. He'd got some girl in the family way but according to Ernie he was doing the honourable thing and standing by her.

A flurry of leaves swirled past the window. Daydreaming had brought her to five past four. It was no longer raining - the balcony outside was protected from the weather anyway - and the sun was glistening off the lawn below.

"I think I'd like to go outside," she told the four o'clock girl. "Get some fresh air."

"Isn't it chilly?" the four o'clock girl asked. "Cold?"

"Just for a moment to clear my head. It's stuffy in this room."

The four o'clock girl's assistant was also there now and they trundled the wheelchair out onto the small balcony.

"Such a lovely tree," said Ellen. "Leaves turning. Look."

From downstairs came a piercing whine. It sounded like the doorbell. It was her, Ellen thought. Her. She had a sudden picture of Megan and took a deep breath.

"Hello, Mrs Pearce!" A voice was addressing her from inside the room, wafting out onto the serenity of the balcony.

Ellen grunted.

"Are you sure you should be out there? It's rather chilly, isn't it?"

"I don't feel it."

"Even so. It's perhaps..."

The carers casting their eyes down appeared sheepish. They had been complicit in Ellen's latest folly.

"I just need to..." announced Josefina.

Too many words all joined into one. What was she supposed to do?

"She needs to come in," Josefina said.
The carers moved towards the wheelchair.
"What do you want me to do?" Ellen asked.
"Stand up," they said.
"But can't I do that here?"
Josefina looked pained and made a note.
"And I need my walking stick," Ellen continued.
"But why?" asked the four o'clock girl. "You never use it."
"I like to have the option," she replied stubbornly.
The stick was handed to her and she placed it to her right.
"Can you stand up, Mrs Pearce?"
The girls were at her elbows, supporting her under her arms. She was slight and light and bobbed up like a cork. Josefina was scribbling away furiously.
"A couple of steps please."
A walking frame was being placed in front of her. Flanked by a girl at each side she took a few paces along the balcony, made a slight semicircle and turned round. She was back in the wheelchair, out of breath yet momentarily exhilarated. She gazed at the overhead lime tree. The girls had vanished. Josefina and clipboard were now at her side.
"On a scale of one to ten how would you...?"
So many questions! She should have asked them before she rose up like some kind of phoenix. Her answers were short, succinct.
"We may have to look at other alternatives," said Josefina, putting down her chart.
A clerk. A mobile clerk. She was only really interested in the papers in front of her, not the girls or even Ellen.
"Perhaps we should go in now," she suggested.
Perhaps we should. In the small space of the balcony, Josefina suddenly went behind to push the wheelchair. Ellen didn't want her to do it; wanted the girls, or better still to have Megan, who really understood.

Quickly she reached out and grabbed the walking stick, afraid it would be left behind.

There was a peculiar cry as Josefina staggered towards the railings and disappeared from sight.

"Oh my god!" said one of the girls downstairs. "She's fallen off the bleeding balcony!"

There was a strangled cry from the hydrangea bush below.

The unexpected appearance of an ambulance at 4 Bebbington Close caused great concern amongst the neighbours, two of whom approached the driver. However, the groaning apparition being wheeled into the van was not that of Ellen Pearce.

"Some woman from the Council, apparently," the driver said.

It was three months later when Ellen experienced the next of her risk assessments. She had not been forewarned so on this occasion there was no time to panic. In any case, she thought, she would be nicer to the injured Josefina, or at least try to. However, above the clipboard at four o'clock was an unfamiliar face.

"Hello. I'm Sonia Bartlett," said the woman and smiled.

"And I'm Ellen," said Ellen.

"I just need you to take one or two steps for me today but in a minute. Take your time."

"Thank you," Mrs Pearce replied.

The door to the balcony was half open, she noticed; the lime tree completely bare.

Sonia's face smiled again. Ellen was ready.

There was no need for the balcony now, she thought. She didn't have 'a bad feeling' about this one. She sailed slowly upwards like a stately ship.

No need for the balcony, she thought, or her walking-stick.

## Cairina Moschata

"It sure is a beautiful place," the ambassador said, looking out across the square.

"I'm glad you like it," said Fred Astley, briefly scratching his nose.

"Forgive me for saying, though, but shouldn't you spell your town with two 'e's? Otherwise, it sounds like a girl's name. My youngest niece is called that."

"We manage," replied Councillor Astley. "And, incidentally, we happen to be a *city*."

"You're kidding!" the ambassador replied. "A small place like this! No way! Is it because of the church you've got here?"

"The cathedral? Why, yes, of course."

"It's kind of weird but I suppose I can handle that. Where *is* the cathedral, by the way?"

"If you just carry along the High Street, it's immediately opposite Argos."

"I might pop in later if there's time."

"It closes at five thirty."

"Thank you."

At that moment a large red-faced duck nonchalantly crossed the High Street.

"Man! There are so many of these things here!"

"The numbers *have* increased slightly."

"I suppose you can always eat them, though they look kind of huge. Looks like some sort of duck."

"I see you're an ornithologist at heart."

"Well... What kind are they?"

"Muscovies."

"Mus*co*vies?" The ambassador put his stress on the second syllable.

"Yes."

"I've not heard of them before. I'm familiar with the mallard."

"I expect you'll see some of them, too."

"Do they take to walking round the streets, too?"

"Not quite in the same way."

"I mean, just *look* at this guy. He seems to be patrolling."

"We've been getting one or two complaints." Councillor Astley was momentarily anxious. "One of the residents down by the river has taken to feeding them."

"Awesome!" gasped the ambassador.

"With the result that they knock on various front doors in the morning waiting and expecting to be fed."

"You don't say!"

"Giving credence perhaps to my daughter's favourite joke."

"A joke?"

"Mummy, there's a man with a bill at the door!"

The ambassador laughed. "That's good!"

"I haven't finished," said the Councillor, slightly peeved.

"It's the way you tell it. Actually, I kind of like it as it is."

The ambassador thought for a moment. Fred Astley wondered if he was counting the cracks in the pavement.

"You'll have to explain the rest of it later," he said.

"Well, perhaps *after* our discussion. If we have time."

"I must say I'm looking forward to this meeting. I usually find them so positive. The interaction."

"That's one way of looking at it."

"I always look on the bright side," the ambassador replied. "Will your P.M be there?"

"You mean M.P."

"No sir. I mean P.M. Mrs Thatcher, I believe."

"Er, no. I'm afraid she retired about twenty years ago. There was a coup."

The ambassador laughed and patted Fred's shoulder. "Just shows you how time flies. You know, I could have *sworn* she was still in charge. I expect you'll be putting up statues all over the place to her."

"Unlikely, I think. Fortunately, she had no connection with this part of the country."

"Fortunately? Isn't that a *little* naughty? What about her great achievements?"

"It's rather a matter of debate. Not everyone sees it the same way."

"There's ingratitude for you! We kind of liked the old bird back home. This neatly dressed dame with her faithful old handbag and husband. She couldn't get enough of Ronnie!"

"Unfortunately, the handbag has not yet retired. It's still in Number Ten."

"Now you've lost me. That's some kind of cryptic meaning. You Brits never really say what you mean."

"I'm Scottish, actually."

"Scottish?" The ambassador paused for a moment. "Well, shouldn't you be up in Scotland, then?"

"Not necessarily. At present, England happens to be ruled by Scots. It's a kind of historical revenge."

"I see. Well, it's good of them. Mind you, Hitler came from Switzerland. That much I *do* know!"

Councillor Astley was too disturbed by the comparison to correct him.

"I think we should head off to our meeting now," he announced, bundling some papers into a bag.

"Are we walking?" the ambassador enquired.

"Yes. It's only at the end of the High Street and round the corner."

There was a pregnant silence.

"Do you mind if we take a cab? My legs are kind of weary."

Fred Astley gaped in surprise at the man who was some ten years his junior. Apart from a protruberance around the belly, he did not appear excessively overweight.

"I'm not sure we could justify the expense. We have to be very careful nowadays. And as we're so near to..."

"Nonsense. If Joe Public can pay for your Home Minister's porn movies, they can surely stump up for a measly cab."

"Not *my* minister, I can assure you. But perhaps in this case..."

"That's more like it!"

Fred Astley stretched out a hand to hail a passing cab. It sailed slowly by and disappeared down the hill.

"We can get one from Market Street."

"How far's that?" asked the ambassador, clearly alarmed. It was not his intention to go trudging round English cities even if they did look like villages.

"Just round the corner. It's halfway to the Council Chambers."

"You wouldn't be making a point there?"

They turned the corner into Market Street where a predatory taxi was waiting. At that moment a red Muscovy waddled across the road.

"There are *hundreds* of these little fellas! What did you call them again?"

"Muscovies."

"It's a strange name. Makes me think of some kind of fish."

"Anchovies, perhaps?"

"That's it. An*cho*vies. My wife Jean keeps putting them in pizzas. She says they're an aphrodisiac but I can't say I've noticed."

*Icarus In Reverse*

They woke the sleeping cab driver, who queried their destination.

"Slip through the doors of my car, mate, and you'll soon be there."

"Drive on!" said Councillor Astley, crossly.

The proliferation of Muscovies and the ambassador's comments were starting to annoy him.

"Man, what kind of accent is *that*?" the ambassador remarked when they were in the back of the taxi. Maybe this guy should see a speech therapist."

Fred Astley wished he could disappear through the crack in the seats, though thankfully the taxi driver remained oblivious to their brief conversation. Around forty seconds later, they were standing outside the monolith of a Council building.

"Looks kind of homely."

"There are plans to move to the edge of town. We need more room, apparently."

"Smart move. That way no one'll get to bother you."

The ambassador was introducing himself to the Chair of the Committee, who had scuttled down the steps to meet him.

"Joseph B. Hubscrauber," he said.

"Barbara Buttsby," said Barbara enthusiastically. Then waving behind her, "This is Mavis Gotobed."

"I'm sure she will," the ambassador guffawed.

There was an uncomfortable silence.

"It's a *local* name," Fred Astley whispered in his ear, as they followed Barbara and Mavis into the meeting room.

"I'm so sorry," the ambassador replied. "All this walking's made me quite light-headed."

"We thought a tour round Council Chambers *before* the meeting and then, if you haven't already been..." Mavis began. She was about to mention the cathedral.

"Sounds awful nice," said Joseph B. Hubscrauber. "But I think I've done enough touring for one day. Whatever it is, could it possibly wait until tomorrow? Though a trip round your lovely Chambers seems just fine."

"There's the video," said Miss Gotobed, "followed by the County Council Experience."

"Now you're spoiling me," said the ambassador. "Though I think I'll take a rain check on the cinema."

"He means wait," Barbara explained to Mavis. She'd been there before.

"Just the tour, then?" said Mavis, a little disappointed.

"Yes, ma'am, if that's okay."

They sauntered past one or two giant portraits on the way to the Debating Chamber.

"Who's this guy?" he asked. "Looks kind of important."

"Oh, that's Councillor Fishguard," said Mavis. "His family used to own a bottling plant near Wiggenhall St. Peter. Or was it Wiggenhall St. German?"

"You have a *saint* called German?" said Joseph B. "And what did he bottle?"

"I'm not entirely sure," replied Mavis. "I think it may have been beer."

"I bet he had a good time in Chambers."

"He was a teetotaller, I believe, said Mavis. "Oh look. There's Councillor Buttsby. She appears to be waving us in."

They wandered into the darkened chamber.

"Looks kind of gloomy," the ambassador remarked.

"The window cleaner'll be coming tomorrow. It's Wednesday," Mavis announced.

"You mean you didn't get him a day early in my honour!"

"Robin will *never* change his day. Tuesday is the Corn Exchange."

"But I thought this *was* the Corn Exchange," tittered the ambassador, but as with an earlier observation, there was little reaction.

Mavis smiled politely.

"How is your hotel? Is it comfortable?"

## Icarus In Reverse

As an exponent of timely distraction, many a Council meeting had been re-routed because of Barbara's expertise. Salient issues of the day were nearly always conveniently forgotten.

"It's a little small, ma'am, and the bed could be bigger. I'll have to ask for King Size next time."

Mavis had a sudden image of the ambassador thrashing wildly about in his bedroom. She blushed violently and hoped that no one would notice in the subdued light of the chamber.

"Well, if you'll excuse me all, I think I should be heading back now. I have a busy day ahead tomorrow."

"Yes, of course," they said.

"Do you know your way back?" Barbara enquired anxiously.

"Yes, ma'am. It seems impossible to get lost in this village."

"We're a city, man," replied Councillor Astley testily after Joseph B. Hubschrauber had left. He paused for a moment. *Why* was he defending the English?

"Never mind, dear," said Barbara. "Think of your blood pressure. Are you still taking the tablets?"

On the way back to the hotel, the visitor somehow managed to take a wrong turn. Taking his eye off the cathedral, which served as a navigational point, he found himself in a secluded square. Feeling his legs gently, which were, after all, unused to such exertion, he sat down on a bench underneath a large lime tree. From there he watched mosquitoes pirouetting in a cloud as they circled gently up and down.

As he glanced to his left, he was aware of something staring back at him. The bird took two steps towards him, sniffed disdainfully and wandered off to the nearest dustbin. Joseph B. Hubschrauber felt slightly disconcerted at the duck's derisory sniff. There was something haughty and dismissive about it as well as being immensely disrespectful to the ambassador's high status.

In the hotel bar he ordered a coke with his evening meal. He sat alone in the wooden-panelled dining room, aware that the staff was unconcerned over their solitary customer. The meal had too many herbs and the garlic, like a persistent councillor, kept repeating itself.

"What's for desert?" he enquired politely.

"Ice cream or posset," said the girl.

"Isn't that some kind of animal?" he ventured.

"I wouldn't know, sir. Animals are usually on the first course," the waitress replied.

Uncertain as to the contents of the posset, he ordered a vanilla ice crowned with a stale tangerine-flavoured wafer.

Later, through his bedroom window, he heard the cathedral clock striking nine o'clock.

In his pyjamas, he bounced up and down on the bed. A new lump had appeared and he wondered whether it could ever be flattened out. The lump wobbled over to the left, then seemed to slide back like a piece of driftwood on an incoming tide.

The radio on in the background was describing some palatial conference in Moscow. In comparison, his visit to the surrounding air bases seemed mundane.

"We are happy," said a voice, "to welcome all eco-representatives to the heroic and celebrated city of Moskva."

A background prompt could be heard followed by a cough.

"I am so sorry. For a moment, I am thinking in my own language. It is, of course, as you know, *Moscow*."

The interview then shifted to a visit to a shoe museum in one of the adjoining suburbs.

It was some moments afterwards that the ambassador made his startling discovery. Moska or Moskva, or whatever it was! Muscovy ducks! There was a connection, surely! The

## Icarus In Reverse

ducks had flown in on one of their oldest allies in an attempt to spy on and possibly destabilise the country! The fact that they were *everywhere*, patrolling the streets, only served to heighten his suspicions. Furthermore, they were likely to be equipped with listening devices to pick up unwitting conversations and vital bits of information as the beasts sauntered casually amongst the unsuspecting citizens.

Then another thought took hold. What if they had got into any of the air bases? It would be typical of some daft wing commander to adopt one of the little roosters as their mascot! Vital secrets could be unwittingly tossed and leaked away when one of these covert and overfed spies waddled past.

Quickly, he reached for the telephone. The voice at the other end appeared unconcerned.

"Is that you, Lambert?"

"You know darn well it is," came the somewhat truculent reply. "When do we expect you back?"

"At the end of the week," said the ambassador.

"And where are you now? I'm afraid I've lost the itinerary."

"Some place in the east U.K. They call it angular, jugular or something."

"Might that be Anglia, sir?"

"It could be. I just can't understand a word these people say."

"A necessary hazard of travel, sir."

"You'd think they were almost doing it deliberately."

"Very likely, sir. And is everything okay back there?"

"Not at all! Which is why I'm calling you. You won't believe it, but the whole village, or city as they like to call it, is overrun by some kind of diabolical duck."

"A what duck, sir?"

"Muscovites or something. If you ask me the Cold War is not yet over!"

"Are you sure, sir?"

"Believe you me. These ducks have some sinister association with Moscow and I reckon they've been fitted out with some kind of listening device. You know how the Russians like to bug everything. They just walk around everywhere, up and down the High Street, even across the Market Square. You can't tell me that's *normal* duck behaviour. They should be sitting in ponds chewing weed."

"But why should that be, sir?" said Lambert in disbelief.

"They're e*verywhere*, I tell you. Patrolling the streets. One even followed me home! There's no place that hasn't been infiltrated. And from closer observation, they don't seem to like water either, which strikes me as highly suspicious."

"It's a duck out of water, then, sir."

"Most certainly. And I should like you to pass on my concerns to the department. Immediately!"

"Your comments have been noted, sir," said Lambert, sounding like an official letter of disinterest.

"These things must have been flown in from the East. Apparently, they weren't here ten years ago. See to it, Lambert, won't you?"

"Yes, Mr. Hubschrauber."

"Thank heavens we still have all our bases!"

"Yes, Mr. Hubschrauber."

"Heaven knows what would have happened if we had given them up."

"Indeed Mr. Hubschrauber."

Lambert put the receiver down and picked up a bottle of mineral water. Speaking on the phone to the ambassador always made his mouth dry.

Later that evening, just before his bedtime reading, Lambert picked up a heavy volume of one of the bird books he had been given for Christmas and which lay neglected along with the other encyclopaedias. His fingers ran over the pages until he came to one marked Cairina Moschata: 'a native of Central America, especially Mexico.'

## Icarus In Reverse

"Well, what do you know?" he exclaimed to himself. "It's from our own back..."

He looked at the ruddy-nosed duck with its puffed-out chest and for a moment it reminded him of someone.

Wondering whether he ought to ring the ambassador back to put an end to his misery and anxiety, he suddenly thought better of it. It could wait till the morning, he decided. Easily wait, and so he switched off the light.

From outside the window came a quack.

# A Variety of Accents

Saturday had finally arrived as Donald Dunstan pulled back his living room curtains. Across the green, a semi-circle of promised tents had duly materialised, their sudden and silent apparition almost as if they had landed from somewhere above. And perhaps they had. Confined to space somewhere between their annual visits. They flapped cheerfully and invitingly in the late spring breeze.

He poured a cup of tea of dubious flavour and gazed through the window. It was better to wait till everything was in full swing. Previous experience had warned him of the acrimonies of preparation. There had been several factions of feuding flower ladies, and, as the fete's fame and lure had now spread to surrounding villages, the sparring had become more volatile and tribal.

At three o'clock, he was ceremoniously opening the garden gate, taking care that it did not swing completely off its hinges, as it so often did, and stepping out onto the soft lush grass of the green. There was the insistent throb of the engine of an ice cream van, so he moved swiftly over to the far side. Here, the tents seemed to flap even more enthusiastically in the nagging breeze, but it was also quieter.

As he gazed beyond the Aunt Sally stall, he noticed for the first time a small new addition to the fete. A diminutive tent announced 'Madame Varga, Balkan Clairvoyant.'

The woman on the dried flower stall was unimpressed. "It's the vicar," she said. "That trendy new one. Says we should go in for 'inclusivity', whatever that is."

## Icarus In Reverse

Donald said he didn't know either but felt it was unwise to prolong the exchange. Madame Varga could be listening and lurking behind the canvas of her flimsy tent. He strolled on in the direction of the tombola stall, manned as usual by Mrs. Hawksley-Woodhouse, and then turned back. Why not, he thought? Why not give it a go?

He remembered once Father O'Malley saying that those who consulted palmists and fortune-tellers would be automatically excommunicated. But these were more enlightened times, surely? And the beneficiary of the annual fete, more often than not, was a church roof, albeit that of a competitor. It would only be a bit of fun.

Mindful of these misgivings, he stepped slightly hesitantly into Madame's tent. It seemed much bigger inside.

"Ah, 'allo, dear," said Varga, in an accent not unlike the one he used to hear in Portsmouth.

"Afternoon," he smiled.

She motioned to him to sit down. "Three fifty, luv," said Varga. "Me overheads is gone up."

What overheads were these, he wondered, as he handed over the money? And what happened to 'cross my palm with silver'? Madame Varga's hand was soft and spongy to the touch. She put the money in a little tin behind her and placed it out of sight under the table.

"I was robbed at the last fete," she said gloomily.

"Oh," said Donald, looking at her dark, expressionless face in sympathy. Surely, as a clairvoyant, she should have foreseen that?

"You are good-looking man," she said, reaching out to take his palm again.

Was this a proposal of marriage, he wondered? He protested unconvincingly and subsided again into the plump, damp fingers.

Maybe West Country Italian, he thought, returning to the accent.

Varga looked at him closely. "Lots of women in your life."

Well, he *was* a teacher and most of his colleagues were…

"Nearby you."

True, thought Donald. There was a church hall used by the Womens' Institute.

It was where he bought most of his jams, but Varga could have surmised this already.

"Your job?" she asked suddenly. "What is?"

Her sentences badly needed reformulating, but he replied, "Teacher. I only do a couple of days a week now."

"You are going on holiday."

Statement or question? It was hard to tell, and yet another trip into the sublimely obvious. Teachers were famous for their summer holidays, weren't they? Currently, they were only two weeks away.

"You have some big test, maybe. Something important."

Yes, exams, they're called, but they've been and gone.

"Coming up."

Well, yes, as a matter of fact, there was a vacancy for a Senior Examiner. He was to be observed and interviewed. He became more interested.

"It is," she scrutinised his hand more carefully, "a little challenge."

He became suspicious again and wanted to withdraw his palm. This was no more than a version of 'footsie' under the table. Clearly insider knowledge; college grapevines.

That's it, he thought. She's a teacher who's seen the interview lists and is able to mimic her students.

"Attention, please!" she barked, sensing a lapse in concentration.

That confirmed it!

"It is…yes… challenging one," she enunciated carefully in less bogus Balkan. "Eat turnip. It will help."

*Icarus In Reverse*

Well there we are, then. My career change is dependent on the consumption of a vegetable!

The interview was over.

"Thank you for your help. It's been most enlightening. I hope it doesn't rain."

"No," she said, looking blankly at him and failing to detect any irony.

He got up, remarking on the largeness of her teeth. They had, in all likelihood, chewed many a carrot in the Dorset area.

"Goodbye, Madame Barker."

"Varga," she insisted.

"Thank you."

"Spassie-ba," she called.

Nice touch of Russian, Donald thought, but you don't fool me.

Two weeks later, they announced the profits from the fete. It had been a resounding success.

"Best year ever!" beamed Mrs. Treadaway.

Then noticing Donald's suit, "You look smart."

"It's a bit of an important afternoon," he replied. "There's a vacancy in the offing."

"Well good luck to you, dear," she said.

"Thank you," he replied. Her confidence was a welcome contrast to the tentative pessimism of Madame Varga. He was going to ask Julia Treadaway if she'd ever heard of her, but time was pressing.

The building, when he got there, was one uniform block. It loomed large and massive, not unlike Bankside Power Station, he thought. He climbed up several flights of steps and into the entrance hall. From there he was directed to a room on the second floor.

"Hello. I'm Mrs. Cuthbertson," said a diminutive figure who had come to speak to him. "I'm Director of Operations."

Operations, thought Donald. He shook hands.

"I've earmarked some lovely students for you. Three super pairs," she cooed. "All of them Swiss."

"You're too kind," he replied.

"And I've got you a *very* nice room."

Donald smiled again.

The high-windowed room looked out onto the Town Hall with its sadly defunct fountain.

"I often used to like looking out at it swooshing away when I was bored in the afternoon," she admitted. "I always thought we should swap buildings. Much nicer for us. Oh, by the way, it'll be Daphne Kirkalcuddy who'll be watching you."

"Fine," Donald said.

"She's a bit of a hippopotamus but otherwise quite friendly. Cup of tea?"

"That'd be nice," Donald replied.

It was at two fifteen when it all started. It began with a muted pair of students who didn't appear to understand each other. On their own, in monologues, they were competent enough. Donald and his co-examiner quickly traded marks, something they were expressly forbidden to do.

"It's better we're seen in agreement, for the first one, don't you think?" asked Maria.

Donald winked.

At that moment, Mrs. Daphne Kirkalcuddy entered, without fanfare, and proceeded to a desk from which she could observe the interviewing techniques of Donald.

"She's a bit deaf," Maria confided to Donald earlier.

"Who is?"

"The hippopotamus."

"Does everyone call her that?"

"Oh yes."

Donald was taken aback. "But how can she know what's going on?"

"I think maybe the higher echelons don't know. If they only communicate by email..."

## Icarus In Reverse

Donald decided to smile at Mrs. Kirkalcuddy, who in turn graciously glowed back.

The second pair of students performed quite capably. They looked into each other's eyes fairly frequently and there was some strange body language.

I wonder if they're having an affair, Donald wondered, and ticked the relevant boxes. He envied his co-examiner, secluded from Mrs. Kirkalcuddy's intrusive eye, safe and secure on her island table of separate assessment.

She didn't have to perform, to entertain or to adhere to meticulous timing. In her free spirit status, Maria suddenly seemed very attractive to Donald.

"Let me look at your marks," she said, comparing Donald's and Maria's sheets. Her eyes floated ominously over the papers for a moment then she returned them with a smile. "Both twenty point five. Yes, you agree nicely."

"I'll send the next pair in," said a voice outside the door. It was an usher.

"Thank you," they said.

"Thank you," Donald repeated. He would gain an extra mark for politeness.

Entering the room now was an extremely tall boy with a smaller dumpier looking girl. She had radiantly, rosy cheeks. They sat down together while Donald introduced himself and wrote down their names.

"I am from a small willage," she began.

"I, too, from a small village," he rejoined.

No verb there, Donald noted, but pronunciation's better. Different from the girl's. French, most likely.

They both agreed that London was very big. The food awful. The weather…well, interesting.

Disagreement was always good for producing language, Donald thought, lapsing momentarily into jargon, but, while placidity reigned, it was unlikely to be happening here.

"And what did you do last weekend?" he asked.

"Oh," said the healthy girl, "I went to some willage. It was celebrate something. Lots of old ladies. It must be typical English."

Donald became unusually attentive. She must mean the fete, he thought. He looked at his script momentarily, but there was nothing that permitted further enquiries on such a subject. What with Mrs. Kirkalcuddy occupying most of the room, he felt it unwise to offer an ad lib question. And what if the healthy girl, Ermintrude, didn't understand the unscripted, then he'd certainly be put on the spot? She would be looking across with a bemused, quizzical eye.

"You deviated from the rubric," she'd say later. "You mustn't!"

This was an unpardonable offence.

Pierre – it was Pierre – was trying to tell him about his family. His rapid breathing and sudden drop of spontaneity suggested that this might be the rehearsed bit, through which one would politely nod.

"My muzzer, she stay at home and cook the dinner."

Lucky her, thought Donald. He saw a woman alone in a fitted kitchen staring out of the window at a herd of forlorn sheep. On the other hand, they might be sympathetic, and he tried to picture a caring and concerned sheep.

"My fazzer, he have a lot of money. In the finance, yes. He work very 'ard."

Ermintrude was nodding in approval.

"He iz an impotent bonker!"

Pierre's last words were sealed with a celebratory triumph while Ermintrude smiled contentedly.

It was the combination of this startling revelation concerning the prestigious financier with the reverie of sympathetic sheep that permitted Donald a nervous staccato giggle. Mrs. Kirkalcuddy glanced up.

The giggle did not end there. Donald, out of the corner of his eye, glanced at his colleague, Maria, who appeared to be chewing the ends of her fingertips and desperately crossing her legs.

Her eyes were deliberately cast downwards and he could see her bosom heaving softly with mirth. She pretended to wipe away something from her eye.

Pronunciation is everything, Donald had once said to a stupefied Monday morning assembly.

And now, with a great guffaw, a hyena-like cackle, the uncertain, tense atmosphere of the room was torn asunder. Tears were rolling down Donald's cheeks. Maria appeared to have swallowed her pencil. The students looked across uneasily at each other, not knowing what to do.

But staring now across the room in horror and disbelief was Daphne Kirkalcuddy. She had not travelled down from Warrington for this! Donald reached for a handkerchief. Mrs Kirkalcuddy reached for her pen. In all probability the remark about Pierre's father and his bank position had passed her by, unnoticed and undetected. What she was not programmed for was laughter, mirth. She got up slowly and, without a word, left the room.

As Donald eventually got up too in the sympathetic silence of both surroundings and Maria, an image came into his mind. He pictured a small row of tents flapping gently in the bright sun of a village green. It was the Saturday when he had first met Madame Varga who hailed from Liskeard, Barnstaple or possibly Swanton Abbot.

As Ermintrude the Swiss candidate had so aptly said, "It was all so …typical…typical English."

# The Preparation

Miss Melchior is wearing red today. In her polo-neck jumper she looks like a giant strawberry as she tentatively leaves the shop.

I say tentatively for there is still ice on the pavements. She turns left out of the door and then left again up the alley. From here she will climb the stairs from the entrance within the passageway and enjoy a ten-minute break.

Her black slacks form a contrast with her red top. She wears no coat today as she ventures outside; a biting wind billowing down the street. It blows a flurry of bus tickets, discarded sweet wrappers, so for a moment, only a moment, it looks like some tickertape procession.

`It is perhaps apt and fitting for a woman of her ability.

She came to the shop a year ago. It had always struggled being in the less fashionable part of town – part bookshop, part gift-shop. Maybe it was unwise to combine the two, indicating a lack of confidence, an identity crisis.

Miss Melchior's hair is never out of place and her make-up is applied with such subtlety that only close examination will tell you that it's there. And customers with enquiries will find she knows *exactly* where each book is, unlike her haphazard assistants. And yet despite conveying such authority, she is *not* the owner. It's a Mr. Caversham who lives in Ripley Vale. He governs in absentia, telephoning in his orders and instructions to Miss Melchior. On occasion, he may visit the shop, too. It's rather like a state visit, I'm told.

## Icarus In Reverse

Finally, Miss Melchior sends for Charlie the window-cleaner. He's quite a young man who nimbly nips up the ladder, and there's his sidekick Dan. I did wonder if they'd be vying for her attention, those two adroit window specialists in their late twenties.

Miss Melchior is forty something, but nevertheless she could well cast an approving eye at the extrovert Charlie. For a while I stopped having them – let my windows go to pot – as I couldn't bear the fact that they enjoyed such ready contact with Serena – Miss Melchior.

However, I needn't have worried, for one evening I was driving along and I passed them coming out of the wood by the river where 'the gentlemen' go. Even from my distant driving seat I could see the tell-tale signs on Charlie's trousers. Dan, wearing more subdued clothing, appeared less exposed. Did they go for each other, I wondered? Or did they merely 'go fishing' together?

I see now that Charlie's macho banter is perhaps all a front and he has no interest in Miss Melchior at all, and that makes me very happy.

I was talking about the 'state visit'. After sending for Charlie, Miss Melchior cleans the insides herself – pale, pink Windolene applied liberally to the fading panes of glass. From both sides now the windows seem to sparkle.

Then she'll arrange a special display – usually cookery books spread in a fan shape or a poster featuring a thoughtful poet. Serena has a good sense of colour and her works of art are quite eye-catching from the street. With the gifts and souvenirs, too, she mounts a competent display, but I suspect her real art is reserved for the books. It is here she displays her 'true love'.

True love.

And then Mr. Caversham arrives unannounced, making a less than dramatic entry in a turned-up overcoat and partly obscured by an umbrella. The dim-witted assistants fail to recognise him even though they must have been primed. Edward Caversham poses briefly as a customer, picking up a paperback before casually wandering towards the counter.

"Would you know anything about this?" he asked the overweight assistant once.

It was my lunchtime. The assistant was chewing gum and I could sense Mr. Caversham's evident distaste.

"Nah, sorry," the assistant replied.

Which is where Miss Melchior glides in. "It's the second book he's published," she says, "though as a sequel it's slightly inferior."

Slightly inferior. That goes for Tweedledum and Tweedledee, who often flank Serena at busy lunchtimes, making her appear ever more a rose among thorns.

I see Miss Melchior locking up the shop, getting off the bus in the twilight suburbs of town. She is the last passenger on board. Some years back, there would have been a conductor with whom to while away the final stages of the ride; the bus emptying, the streets more deserted – orange soda lights against a darkened sky. But now there is no conductor, just a tired driver cocooned behind a plastic case. We live in a world of fear and safety.

Miss Melchior mutters her thanks to the driver but I am sure they are not reciprocated. Her voice may not be heard against the juddering vehicle that has still not quite come to rest. It will turn back on itself, ready to make the return journey into town.

Miss Melchior quickens her footsteps in the darkened streets. She will soon be home. The road she lives in tapers upwards; houses of varying anonymity. She will take off her coat in the hall, hanging it neatly on the hooks above the telephone. At that moment she reaches out to turn on the light switch.

But there will be no light today. She tries again and it is then that her nose will start to twitch slightly, delicately.

*Icarus In Reverse*

An invisible trail of aroma will release itself beneath the kitchen door. She will stop for a moment in surprise, trying to wonder what it might be. She will recount her past recipes and find that none of them match.

She will head quickly towards the kitchen now for the matches that can be found in one of the large drawers beside the sink. And as she opens the door to the kitchen with its adjoining sitting room, she will gather her first impression. Confused at first with all the flickering candle lights that make both rooms seem like a dream.

The table is perfect – all prepared – the casserole still bubbling in the oven.

It is then she takes full stock of all the preparation, all my hard work.

And for some reason, she screams.

# Codpiece

"Bananas," said Guy. "Absolutely bananas."

"I'm sorry," said Connie, holding the receiver to her ear. "I can't hear very well. Let me turn the radio down."

There was a scrunching sound as she subdued the radio, a rustling like rain on rooftops and the bickering voices of Radio Four were silenced. She picked up the receiver again, noticing she had left a butter thumbprint from a piece of toast. Guy always seemed to ring at awkward times; the inconvenience invariably heightened by a sense of drama. He had, after all, been a part-time thespian.

"It's Hilltop," Guy announced. "And this time it's bananas."

Ah, Hilltop, thought Connie. The well-known exam board for whom they both worked, and longer than they cared to remember. In the early summer months, Connie's Morris Minor would be meandering down winding lanes in search of obscure venues and newly established language schools.

"It's nice to hear from you, Guy."

Guy Lambert did not reciprocate. He was too far gone.

"Supermarket receipts," he frothed, adding another twist to the cryptic puzzle.

This time Connie was with him. The speaking examiners who trundled far and wide summer and winter were able to claim a single meal allowance. This was something Connie always did and often feasted on the homely fare provided by

*Icarus In Reverse*

the Bull and Gate which was handily situated at the bottom of her lane.

Lately, with the closure of pubs and the sudden disbanding of restaurants, her colleagues had been visiting supermarkets – which were in no small way responsible for the demise of drinking and eating establishments – and handing in till receipts. Connie reached for her mug of hot tea, its last wisps of steam slowly evaporating over the breakfast table.

"I'm increasingly fed up," said Guy.

"You were talking about receipts," she reminded him. At alarming tangents Guy would go off in quest of other tales and events. At times he was the Tristram Shandy of the telephone world.

"I'm coming to that," he retorted.

A trifle tartly, Connie thought, and at such a tender hour in the morning! Her grandson, were he staying with her, would not be up for another six hours yet, surfacing halfway between lunch and tea and gaping incredulously at the dining room clock as if it were still too early.

Teenagers needed their sleep. Only the previous morning the Today Programme had provided an apologia for idle youth and a Doctor Winkelstein was vigorously propounding his views.

"I went to Cressco to spend my allowance," Guy continued. "I'd been examining over at Parsons Green so it was quite late when I returned. Give them their due, though. They did provide a lovely plate of sandwiches at lunchtime."

"I'm so glad," replied Connie. She was missing the radio, the inexorable drift towards Desert Island Discs.

"So I went in," Guy continued, "and bought a Macaroni Cheese."

Why on earth would anyone buy *that*, Connie thought? It could so easily be concocted at home. A way of using up irritating leftovers before they acquired blue mould.

"I had sixty pence left over from the allowance," he announced.

Connie was busily working out how much the Macaroni Cheese must have cost. In any event it was far too expensive.

"So I fancied a pudding. Well, a banana, in fact."

The same radio programme had also warned that bananas were likely to be extinct in the not too distant future. They were having problems reproducing themselves, or something like that. Guy was perhaps wise to invest in their availability.

"And there was this offer on. A BOGOF."

"Oh yes," said Connie.

"The bananas were quite delicious. Not too firm. They often sell them too green and it takes an age to ripen them in this weather."

"I put mine on the windowsill," suggested Connie, helpfully.

"But not too ripe either," said Guy, ignoring her. "A quite remarkable texture."

A remarkable texture. An endangered fruit, thought Connie. A world without tigers or bananas.

"And then this morning I've had a letter."

"A letter?"

"Yes. From Hilltop. In the letter they state that in *their* opinion 'one banana should suffice'...not three."

Was Guy a vegetarian, Connie wondered? From the intimacies of his till receipts, he could well be. And could not the bananas have been claimed for culinary purposes? A curry perhaps or a quasi vegetable dish a la plantain?

"Well, I was *furious*," said Guy. "I'm writing straight back. It was the same price as for *one* banana! And who are *they* to question my eating habits?"

"Yes," said Connie. There was little answer to that and if Guy were to permit her the right to reply it would have to be squeezed between his next indignant outburst.

"It could have been worse, I suppose."

## Icarus In Reverse

"How so?" Guy challenged.

Did he think she was defending Hilltop?

"I was referring to the letter of omission. You know, when the examiners forget to fill in the marksheets."

"Ah yes," said Guy, comprehending.

The cardinal sin, the gravest error, when examiners, for various reasons, failed to complete the oval, rugby-style lozenges. It defeated the object in many ways. Connie pictured miscreants being bundled into mysteriously dark limousines, flanked by intimidating heavies and then taken away for questioning.

"I'm not letting them get away with it," Guy repeated. "It's not as if they're financially disadvantaged."

"Hardly."

"And the expense in pursuing this is clearly far greater. Time, paper, heating, administration!"

Clerks, thought Connie. Clerks. More people were killed by clerks. Great dictators were usually types of clerks. Bureaucratic executioners never directly involved in the fray.

"I should have a nice cup of tea first," she remarked. "And then write."

She manoeuvred slowly with her cordless phone, tiptoed to the front door and carefully undid the latch. Groping outside with her free hand, she pressed the welcome dimple of her doorbell. It rang alarmingly loudly so that even Guy at the other end, deep in monologue, would have jumped.

"Is that your bell?" he asked.

"Yes, I think so," said Connie, creeping back into the house.

"It sounds quite urgent."

"You may be right, dear."

"I'll leave you to it, then," said Guy, magnanimously.

"Best of luck," wished Connie.

Connie was motoring back from Dawlish Towers, a boarding establishment by the sea, from which the pupils, surrounded also by fifteen miles of empty, undulating countryside had little chance of escape. It had gone quite nicely and she was fairly happy to meander at five miles an hour behind an alarmingly swaying tractor along country lanes which provided little opportunity to overtake. In between watching the wobbly end of the tractor as it swung violently around a corner, she pictured Freda Turner's enticing steak and kidney pie at the Bull and Gate. Her suet pastry melted in the mouth and there was often broccoli and carrots.

The tractor continued its journey for another six miles during which Connie became hungrier and hungrier; hungrier still when she saw the welcome sign of the pub squeaking in the wind. It was quieter than usual when she entered; subdued almost. Something was different.

"Bloody power cut," said Sid. "Food's off."

"Oh," said Connie. "What a shame."

"Ale's not affected, though," said Sid reassuringly, patting the bottom of a set of handpumps. When he was not doing this he was patting Freda's bottom.

Connie declined. She could not contemplate a pint without Freda's pastry. She politely said her goodbyes to Sid, who was staring morosely into space, and walked back to the comfort of her car. What was she to do? She had been wrong-footed. There was now a pressing if not urgent need for food. On turning left at the mini-roundabout, she noticed that the lights of the corner supermarket were still on.

Feeling ever so slightly a betrayer of Sid, she tiptoed inconspicuously to the frozen food counter. Heavy layers of frost concealed many burgers. There was also O'Leary's double lasagne and something unidentifiable. She reached instead for the security of fish. Undoing the layers of wrapping on the kitchen table, she noticed that a second box had somehow been included. Leaving the spare one on the garage window ledge above the small freezer, she ran back inside to set the oven. It took an age to cook, not helped by her

## Icarus In Reverse

frequent anxious inspections and tentative openings of the oven door.

Finally, at nine thirty, the fish appeared ready. It was a dismal affair; soggy and limp in the middle, a sad recompense for Freda's pie, her ready smile and a glass of Old Peculier.

Connie went to bed an hour later and dreamed of a sinister, sliding octopus.

It was one month later when she heard it drop onto the mat. She picked up the leaflet from the Baptist Church along with the large, brown envelope. Taking it to be a last minute assignment, she put on her reading glasses. In disbelief, she stared at the wording. It wasn't possible. A reprimand. A reprimand! The till receipt she'd sent them – and it was the first time she had indulged in such a thing – showed 'excessive disproportion.' Disproportion!

'In the circumstances' the letter continued, 'we feel that *one* portion of crispy cod fillet with lemon goujons should suffice.'

Connie sat down mortified. A letter! It was now she truly understood the nature of Guy Lambert's distress, which had perhaps been met on her part with insufficient concern or sympathy. A wretched sensation came over her. The colours evaporated from the morning.

Her 'fish fillet claim would be met on this occasion but in future...'

Had she really bought two? Perhaps in that loathsome fish cabinet they had got stuck together and in her hunger, her eagerness to get out of the over-lit supermarket, she had failed to notice. She blamed the power cut, the careless farmers that were always cutting through cables as they ploughed to the very edge of their fields, and the subsequent loss of Freda's steak and kidney pie.

Picking up the cordless phone, she dialled Guy's number, suddenly overcome by a wave of guilt as to how she had terminated their last conversation and her use of the doorbell deception. She needed to speak to him, to elicit sympathy, to share her sense of distress. There was no reply. Guy was no doubt out somewhere, enjoying the delights of suet pastry and in a place superior to Freda's. She looked at the time. It was eleven o'clock. Far too early, of course. She rang again and this time the answering machine clicked in. Connie beat a hasty retreat.

At five thirty, after a miserable afternoon, the phone tinkled softly.

"You rang?" said a voice, sounding like the butler.

"Guy!"

She sounded pleased.

"I've had a letter, Guy."

"A what?"

She explained.

"I'm not surprised," said Guy. "After all the problems I had with those bananas!"

He proceeded to narrate the experience again.

"Yes, Guy. You *told* me!"

He carried on regardless. He was in full flow. She wanted to talk about her fateful fish but all he could do was relate his tale of the banana.

"Goodbye, Guy," she said finally, wishing she had again recoursed to the doorbell ploy.

Connie took a stroll out into the garden. There was the comfort of the two laden apple trees between which the washing line was strategically placed.

She had just completed her wander when she noticed something through the garage window. Stepping inside there was an immediate pungent smell. Walking round the now dormant Morris Minor, she could see no tell-tale leak of oil.

And then she glanced over towards the shelf above the freezer. There was an abandoned bag, and in it, triangular and forlorn, the forgotten fish, the neglected partner of the

*Icarus In Reverse*

BOGOF deal. She needed to open a window as the garage was rife with the disintegrating remains of cod.

What a waste, she thought, as she held it at arm's length above the welcome reach of the dustbin. Not just a waste but a misery too, for this had been the unwitting cause of her censure and rebuke. As she held the fish above the gaping hole, she suddenly hesitated. It did not drop.

In an instant, she replaced the lid.

Taking the fish inside, she let the surplus moisture dribble down the sink from its shiny and sweaty packaging. Then she dried it with her least favourite tea towel. It took her only a few moments to compose the letter of contrition. In the large A4 envelope that was to house it, she placed the fish inside.

Later that evening she recalled the last few sentences to an unusually attentive Guy Lambert.

'In view of my miscalculation and my considered eagerness not to upset the members of the examining board, I am returning the extraneous fish. I trust you will pardon an oversight which was, in part, caused by the unavailability of my normal reading glasses and the earlier disappointment of Freda Turner's steak and kidney pie, which, in turn, had been adversely affected by a power cut, which was probably caused by...'

Connie cleared her throat. He did not laugh exactly, but in the unusual silence she thought she could detect the vague flicker of a smile.

# Widdershins

I have a new lover on Sundays. Unforeseen. Quite by chance.
    I had ambled into the church hall in the expectation of architecture but it was damp and depressingly dull. It smelt of stale tea and biscuits and there was another odour reminiscent of armpits. I pictured a ladies' yoga class taking place, the tables cleared away and prayer-like exercise mats dotted like lozenges on the harsh wooden boards.
    But just as I was turning away, I bumped into him. A sombre shadow with a white rim at the top. No wonder he was invisible in this Stygian gloom.
    "I'm so sorry," he began, though it was clearly my fault. I was thinking about the Halesworth Imp and whether I had missed it on my tour of the interior.
    "No, no," I said and apologised too. We were already on the mutual altar of forgiveness.
    I noticed the dark hairs of his hand and saw that they matched those of his slightly inclined head. He might be a good listener... for a man.
    "I didn't see the Gnome," I explained.
    "Ah, of course."
    It was enough to make him stop what he was doing, carry the last pile of cups towards the empty hatch and ask me to follow him. He turned to the left when we stepped outside, the sunlight blinding now after the darkened hall.
    "Could we go this way?" I suggested, pointing to the right.

## Icarus In Reverse

It could have been seen as a quirk, a foible, a division of great political significance.

"Widdershins," I said.

He was none the wiser, appeared puzzled and smiled at me.

"I like to walk round clockwise," I explained. "For the outside, that is. Anti for the interior."

I could have been speaking Serbo-Croat.

"Widdershins?"

"Against the shine. The sun. It's Anglo-Saxon, I believe."

He was clearly no scholar but in the sunshine he seemed younger, more handsome.

"It's unlucky. Or so I've been told."

I couldn't remember who told me but it served a purpose. He was mesmerised.

"If you walk round anti-clockwise, around the building, well it's widdershins, which means against the shine."

I expected him to be scornful of any superstition, of my admission of paganism, but he nodded and said 'Fascinating.'

Afterwards he showed me his Imp or the Gnome as some call it. It was quite easy to miss, buried under a plinth on one of the more robust pillars.

"We used to light it up," he said, imparting an image of community, of faithful flock. "But they pinched all the light bulbs. We think it might have been Flora but we can't be sure."

I admired his candid admission and had a fleeting vision of Flora, somehow large, curly-haired, solid as a tub of margarine, but with a huge collection of electric light bulbs spread ceremoniously on the sacrificial kitchen table.

I wanted to reach out and console him, comfort him for his loss, but we are not a tactile race, and even less so Anglican vicars, apart from the trendy ones who are highly suspect.

But the chance came moments later when we stepped outside, again into a sudden rush of sunlight, for I was temporarily dazzled and misjudged the rising turf. It was still wet and sticky after an earlier shower.

"Ooh!" I gasped.

Then came the proffered hand. I heard a theme from a Tchaikovsky overture – Romeo and Juliet no doubt – and I arose in slow motion like a resurrected galleon.

He invited me back to the vicarage for tea and there we are...

So I have a new lover on Sundays as Monday is his day off and so he stays over. I can see his bike over on the hill, outlined against a dramatic sky. It makes me think of a Bergman movie where they end up playing chess.

He does not stay the other days. Devotion to duty, his flock, and there may be an ex-wife drifting in there somewhere, although he doesn't say.

And I for my part am more than happy with the arrangement. Sunday had always been rather dull – until now. When we meet headlong on the kitchen table, which is his favourite position, I surmise he is a baritone, especially when he calls out 'Kitty!'

And I, of course, have lovers for other days, so I don't long for company. Living where I do there are always the murderous jealousies of the countryside. And Oxfordshire is possibly the homicidal capital of the world. I can see them eliminating each other ruthlessly in Cluedo-style murders where the favoured venues are the conservatory or the library.

And I am powerless to stop it.

*Icarus In Reverse*

# Birdsong

In my room there is no clock so everything is silent. I asked about it the day I came, when I first came into the room.

"No clock, dear," they said. "No clock, Elsie."

I could have sworn it was packed in the suitcase, the brown one that Harold used to bounce up and down on to get shut.

"Be careful," I said. "Be careful of the clock."

He was a little impatient as he always is. Gerry is different. Gerry is placidity itself. But Harold it was doing the packing.

"No clock, dear," they said. "No clock."

"We'll get another," Harold said when he came back later.

"I wanted *that* clock. The small carriage clock. For me, it's company and besides Arthur gave it me.

It's getting dark outside and I shall soon be going to the cinema. The parking space will disappear and darkness will creep over the lawns, spilling over like a great big soup. When it gets really dark, a light appears outside and I turn towards the window, to that gap in the curtains and beyond.

It's a bright sunny day and we're all sitting on the grass. Long before I met Arthur. There's Aunt Emily and Twig and they're opening a picnic hamper. Birdsong all round. Different calls and cries. I know them all. It's easy when you know. You recognise one and then you build on that. From chaffinch over to carrion crow.

Someone comes in and passes me a cup of tea only it's not in a cup but a plastic beaker with a lid. I'm annoyed because they disturbed me. Disturbed me when I was sitting on the grass. The tea is lukewarm. It tastes sweet and soapy but Emily and Twig have cleared everything away. I didn't get a sandwich, though.

Someone comes to see me. I haven't seen them before. She says her name is Penny and I say... She has a pen and paper. She likes writing because all the time I'm talking she's jotting away.

"Are you the secretary?" I ask.

She smiles then laughs. "No, Mrs Soper."

I look around. The name's familiar. I talk some more. I tell her about Emily and Twig and she glances up for a moment, her head turning to one side like a bird's. From chaffinch to carrion crow...

I look outside but there are no birds now and I wonder if the cat has crossed the lawn. She carries on writing and asks me what I do.

"I'm a secretary, just like you." I say. "Worked for Fodder and Fodder. Various things."

I stop for a moment and think about the name. Why repeat it? Why Fodder *and* Fodder? And why Fodder? It's not a very nice name when all is said and done. Fodder is for chickens and animals. Fodder and Fodder.

She asks me if I'm comfortable here and I laugh. 'Are you sitting comfortably? Then I'll begin.' But first there was the music.

Only she *has* begun – still writing.

I've had enough now. I want it to get dark. I want to go out and go to the cinema.

They wheel me into a room where I have some more sloppy food. It's runny and doesn't stay on the plate. Fodder. Not as nice as the picnic I went to yesterday. Emily and Twig. Birdsong. Chaffinch.

## Icarus In Reverse

They put on the television, which is running up the wall. People in front of boxes answering questions. Stupid questions. I don't want it on. I don't! I don't!

I yell as if I've been stung by a wasp. They hide inside the fallen apples when you pick them.

They come in now and turn the television off. It's quiet – getting dark. Slowly the light appears beyond the curtains and I'm out in the street with Arthur. He holds my arm. Such a nice touch. A warm touch. He smiles at some of the ladies going by; touches his hat. I like to be on his arm because I'm sailing gently down the street. I can't feel my feet on the pavement even. He smiles at me and I think how gentle he is. How soft his touch. On and on we walk, leaving the town behind.

They come in now with a cup of tea and Arthur's gone. I look around. No clock. No carriage clock. I feel far too sleepy and some plastic thing bounces to the floor.

Next morning, after a dry, congealed egg, two of them come to see me.

"Elsie," they say. "You've been accepted."

Accepted? Who accepted me?

And then I remember that's what Brian said one afternoon.

"Mum," he said. "I've been accepted."

He held up the letter with the college stamp. I felt so proud and kissed the smoothness of his cheek.

"Leave off!" he said. But he kissed me back later.

They're interrupting me. Interrupting. Always!

"To Chettisham Lodge."

Chettisham Lodge? I've never heard of it. It sounds like a spa or a country house or a ...

"You'll be going Monday."

They smile. One of them squeezes my hand.

"We'll be sorry to see you go."

Sorry? Well, if you're sorry, why should I go, then?

Chettisham Lodge?

I should ask the secretary, the one who came and wrote down all those things.

"A woman," I say. "A secretary. I remember now."

"Yes," says the one who squeezed my hand. "From Chettisham Lodge. They came to see you! They've accepted you."

It sounds like some kind of prize.

I'm travelling in a little blue van. It's grey and white inside and the driver has a dark uniform. The hand squeezer's with me too.

"Nice to be out," she says. "Lovely day. So sunny."

I look through the windows and see the trees passing by but there are no birds to be heard from here.

They wheel me through a long hall and show me an empty room.

"This is yours," they say. "We'll put up your things later."

A final squeeze of the hand and she's gone.

But they still didn't find my clock. It's lying somewhere undiscovered.

And now evening comes. It's quiet. I wait. It's dark. I keep waiting.

But this time there's nothing behind the curtains. There are no lights, no picnics. Nothing.

This time it's all gone.

# New Wave

I suppose it was rather an impressive sight, all those boats and barges straddling the river. But, to be honest, I'd rather have it with nothing at all. Just an empty swathe of mighty, virile water.

There, I'm thinking about sex again. I mentioned 'virile' and 'straddling'. One does when one gets slightly bored. And bored I was. All those boats hooting, tooting, chugging and groaning, and to tell you the truth my arm was getting a tiny bit tired. All that waving. I've been waving all my life and now they were wanting to celebrate sixty years of waving! Proper waving.

You see, *I* didn't. Twenty five was quite nice. Although when the first one happened there was the name of that rude group called the Sex Rifles. Sex again, you see.

Then came fifty. Not bad either. But then ten years later, and seemingly in the twinkling of an eye, the next one. We're at it again!

One of the grandchildren recorded some of it – the last one – on a taping machine. I listened to the commentary and was ...well, truly appalled. Such banality! Such triteness! And so my heart went out to the *whole* nation for having to listen to such twaddle. I have to say I fell asleep and it took them quite a while to revive me.

So that was when I started having doubts about the diamond one. But what could I do? Abdicate? Unthinkable! Besides we all remember the last time *that* happened. That dreadful uncle and the odious American woman! Of course I wasn't exactly happy with the 'boy' here. And I'm not really sure I want that horsey woman being where she shouldn't. I've never quite understood his fascination with it.

Naturally the old man had the best solution. Blamed it on a bladder infection and buggered off to hospital. I wondered why he was pouring his cranberry down the sink. It's not so long since he was *last* in.

I shouldn't be surprised if he had the 'hots' for that nurse from Liverpool. Pretty little thing though I can't understand a word she says. *He* doesn't seem to mind. Just smiles and says 'Carry on.' And so she does and they do.

Are you still with me? I hope you're not too shocked. I have to admit one dozed off just for a few minutes during the flotilla. I awoke, or so I thought, and imagined that all the boats before me were the Spanish Armada. Trying to get one over you see! Only for a moment, though. 'Sound the cannons,' I wanted to cry and then I realised that was the prerogative of my forebear. Such a cultured lady. No kids. The first one, I mean. She lasted a long time, too, you know. Wise and steely. Though naturally not as long as great, great granny!

Both of them had a strong libido, apparently. I was reading that book by the TV chef, Mr. Freud. I didn't know he did psychology as well, though somebody said it was his granddad.

Oh well, it's nearly over. They're putting on some pop concert in the evening. As if I hadn't suffered enough! But I've got these little things to put in my ear. One of the grandchildren again! And it's discreetly wired up to Radio Four. I'm told it's all about begonias on Gardener's Question Time this week. I'm doing the 'Listen Again' thing so I shan't miss anything of course.

And while I listen I shall wave. Wave, wave. Constantly waving!

*Icarus In Reverse*

# Ultimate Predictions

"Forty seconds!" frothed Henry when he came in. "Forty bloody seconds! It's an insult!"

Milly looked up sympathetically. "Don't get yourself worked up, dear. Come and sit down and have a cup of tea. Then you can tell me all about it."

"That's your answer to everything, isn't it," he replied testily.

"Can you think of anything better?" Milly asked him.

He shook his head. "Forty seconds between four countries! England, Scotland, Wales, and..." He paused for a moment. "What's the other one?"

"The Isle of Man," said Milly. "We're not getting onto Northern Ireland again."

"Precisely," replied Henry. "Well, that makes it five."

"So what's been going on, then?" Milly asked. "I've never seen you so peeved."

"Peeved?" he retorted. "Peeved? I'm bloody furious! I mean, to be surreptitiously sidelined like this."

"I'm still none the wiser," moaned Milly.

"It's like this. The weather used to come on at five to eight. Then they decided to chop two minutes off. Okay. Fair enough. We could live with that, though it did mean the speed of delivery had to be...well, enhanced."

"You mean gabbled, dear. It's okay. You don't need to mince words with me. I'm for the robustness of truth. Always have been. It was being married to Arthur all that time. Very blunt, he was. Comes with having an outside toilet. Especially in winter."

Henry looked at Milly for a moment. The connection was slightly lost on him.

"Then from the three minutes of weather for the three, four or possibly five countries came the pruning."

"Pruning?"

"They started overrunning. Interviews with those people who never listen to anyone went over."

"You mean politicians, dear."

"Exactly. And then at the end, they cut the forecast short to tell you what's coming on next. Other programmes later on in the day!"

"I suppose they want to keep the listeners interested," suggested Milly.

"But in *my* slot! At three minutes to eight! When the whole nation is listening with bated breath."

"It sounds lovely the way you say it."

"People in traffic queues, choking on Corn Flakes – it's what they used to give chickens in the war, by the way – reaching out for me under the covers..."

"To turn you on, you mean?"

Henry ignored her. "They reach out all over the country and what do they get? Forty seconds of truncated, often incoherent information delivered at the speed of a 78 gramophone record."

"We never had a gramophone," lamented Milly.

Henry took a large swig of tea which failed to placate him. "What *is* to be done? I mean, to make way for *programme advertising*! The present ignominiously sacrificed for the future. It's the *future* that ruins us all. Look at all these bloody targets they've given us now. The country's obsessed!"

"Hmm," said Milly unconvinced. "I thought the weather was all about the future. It is a forecast after all."

*Icarus In Reverse*

"With our improved accuracy," said Henry, "it is less of a prediction, more a statement. Look at *my* record."

"Impeccable, probably," said Milly. "Guaranteed weather with Henry Hargrave."

"There you have it. It was not I who failed to predict the great hurricane of '87 when Aunt Mathilda's walnut tree was blown down."

"I'm very fond of walnuts," said Milly. "So you mean, had she known, she could have done something about it?"

"Precisely."

"Like what?"

"Batten down the hatches. I don't know...Something. How anyone can miss a hurricane is beyond me! Even the *French* spotted it!"

"Ah well."

"Ah well, what?"

"We have to be different, don't we? Always have been. Because *they* spotted it, I suppose we couldn't. Act as if it wasn't there."

"We had to keep a stiff upper lip. Is that what you're saying? Well, the fact remains I have never failed to predict a hurricane."

"Perhaps they don't appear on your shift," suggested Milly.

"What do you mean, don't appear?"

"Anyway, I felt sorry for the chappie. Such a lovely man. A homely sort of person. Nice moustache."

"This is radio not TV we're talking about! It's quite a different kettle of fish."

"That's his name!" exclaimed Milly. "Michael Kettle. A lovely man. Always so cool and relaxed."

"So relaxed that he missed the bloody hurricane!" retorted Henry. "And from which time the profession seems to have been placed under a cloud. And then slowly, very slowly, they started chipping away at us. What will happen to the forty seconds? What if they start using jingles?"

"It could be nice at Christmas."

Henry shuddered briefly.

"But surely not?" continued Milly. "That's for the other radio stations."

"But what if it comes here? It's only a matter of time. They will hack away even further. The weather will be reduced to a one liner. It might even be spoken by someone else."

"Oh, Mister Henry!" she exclaimed. "I couldn't bear that! For you and all those lovely weather men to be replaced. And specially that new lad Chris. He's ever so young. Wears the nicest shirts."

"I'm afraid the listeners may be unaware of his wardrobe."

"They can sense it, you know. They can build up a picture from the voice."

They looked at each other across the table.

"So what is to be done, then, Milly? What's to become of us who...?"

"Say no more, Mister Henry," she said. "I have an idea."

That evening Henry couldn't settle. He had not blown his fuse properly in the conversation with Milly as there was still a residual nagging, an irritation bubbling away. Even videos of Little House on the Prairie did little to assuage his increasing resentment.

Prairies, he thought. I shouldn't be condoning them by watching them. A very adverse effect on weather, not to mention the countryside.

He watched the latter part of the news from a rival TV company, feeling that his affiliations to his own employer were now sorely tested. As the news concluded, there was a sudden, abrupt jingle and he found he was staring at a rival weather forecast.

## Icarus In Reverse

"Southern Weather," it announced," brought to you by E.P.Dawkins & Co; Plumbing Installations whatever the weather."

Behind what looked like a souwester and mackintosh, the presenter dolefully intoned what lay ahead for the week.

"Of course," said Henry. He remembered now that rival TV dressed their presenters up according to various climatic conditions.

Thank heavens it's not summer, he thought. The prospect of the gawky Brian le Saux dressed in a swimsuit was enough to put anyone off their evening meal. There were definitely advantages to radio broadcasting, he concluded.

But then as Brian expanded into his fourth minute on air, full of jovial asides, the odd truncated anecdote, a twinge of jealousy grabbed Henry.

Four minutes! Unheard of! The unimaginable luxury of being able to *explain* the complexities of occluded fronts, the inconsistencies of high pressure.

Then suddenly a caption of a flush lavatory appeared, followed by another eulogy to E.P.Dawkins &Co, performed by a talking toilet seat, to the magnanimous benefactors who had generously sponsored the broadcast 'whatever the weather'.

Why did weather need sponsoring, he thought? Did it need some kind of encouragement or financial support? Was it supposed to make a profit perhaps, and if so, how? And why, he thought, should the installation of flush toilets and washbasins, which were normally inside the house, be affected by meteorological conditions?

No, it was all wrong, he decided. Patently absurd. Four minutes thirty five seconds – he'd been counting – for the bedraggled Brian le Saux, whereas for his colleagues and himself a mere forty seconds was all that was allocated. He made himself a cup of cocoa and trotted petulantly off to bed.

His dreams were strange and interwoven. At one point he was at a fair, eating candy floss, which for no reason bubbled up into a pink cloud. The cloud went rapidly into orbit taking Henry with it in its swift ascent. From his remote and lofty perch he was able to observe the impending Atlantic fronts bubbling up beneath, while on an adjoining cloud, complete with angels, celestial harp and cymbals, Milly was shrilly and vigorously singing to him. Why she should be engaging in this serenade was unclear. Henry felt the sides of his cheeks to check his fillings had not been damaged. Milly, displaying her usual thoughtfulness, relinquished her top Cs.

Her mood was enthusiastically upbeat; she smiled and waved to the attendant seraphim, proclaiming "Ev'rythin's gonna be alright!"

Henry awoke the next day with something approaching a hangover. The TV broadcast sponsored by the enterprising Dawkins, combined with Milly hallelujah-ing from some kind of Cirrus Stratus, did not rest easily with him. He burnt the toast, which, in turn, set off the smoke alarm. Unable to silence its insistent shrieks, which were on a par with Milly's, he completed his breakfast in the relative sanctuary of the bathroom, whose forlorn interior was clearly crying out for that little bit of E.P.Dawkins magic.

He reached for his battered raincoat and left the house. The dismal mood persisted with him all the way to work and beyond. Barely acknowledging the radio station's burly security guard, he made his way forlornly to the staff room and opened his locker.

"Morning Mister Henry." Milly greeted him with a more than radiant smile.

He grunted a reply.

"Oh dear," said Milly. "Someone's got out the wrong side of bed."

As Henry's narrow bed was hemmed in on one side by a gigantic wardrobe, he had little option. Besides, he failed to understand the meaning of this saying. Was there a right side? And if so, which one was it and how could you identify it?

"Someone's cheerful," he grudgingly acknowledged.

"Me, dear?" she replied. "You know me. Start of the working day. Always happy. Feel as if I'm on Cloud Nine!"

"Pardon?" Henry stared at her suspiciously and as he did so a jar of pickled walnuts fell out of the locker. The dream sequence came flooding back, not least Milly's inescapable wailing from her aerial perch. He rescued the jar with a pained expression.

"Are you all right, dear?" she asked. "Lumbago not playing you up again?"

"I'm perfectly fine," he replied.

"If you say so."

"I do."

Milly rattled the tea cups on her ever ready trolley. He was about to enlist her sympathy on the needless luxury of the programme time afforded to Brian le Saux but thought better of it.

However, as if reading his thoughts, Milly said softly, "You shall once again achieve your aim, Henry Hargrave."

He turned round to look at her. She was clearly talking nonsense, he thought. The solo on the cloud had obviously gone to her head.

"And how is that ever going to be likely?" he asked her sadly.

"Just leave it to me, dear. I know what's bothering you and I'm going to sort it out."

"Yes, of course." He had no idea what she was on about.

He gratefully downed one of her more potent cups of tea as the trolley purposefully meandered through the department.

"What's this?" he said, gazing at the pink sheet of paper he had found in the in-tray.

"Mission statement," she said. "Boss's orders. Everyone's got to have one."

"Such nonsense," he said and prepared himself for his forty-second broadcast by gargling with a variety of mouthwashes.

"I think you'll find it useful," she said.

It was two minutes to go before he was on air. For some reason, he felt oddly nervous, as if a whiff of expectancy had seeped into the otherwise cosy and compact studio.

"Three minutes to eight," a sombre voice intoned.

The producer waved his arms in a silent gesture more usually associated with air hostesses.

As Henry sped through most of Northern England, he noticed the directing hands becoming more languid, as if urging him to slow down. Astonishingly, they had already breached the minute mark!

And so it continued. Another card urged him to slow down over the Eastern Counties of Scotland and a variety of contrasting temperatures popped up onto the screen. A combination of conflicting weather fronts was responsible for these wildly fluctuating variations, he explained.

He was into two minutes now and still going strong. A spring had gathered in his verbal step and being permitted to flex his vocal muscles for longer than usual, he exulted in a confident and exuberant rhythm. There was time for a short anecdote about Miss Wilkinson's broody hen as his attention turned to the Wash. Two minutes! He couldn't believe it! Couldn't remember the last time he had been so free and uninhibited! With a triumphant spout of saliva, he ran for a whole three minutes up to the meaningful and declamatory pause before the' Pips'.

Henry sat down in triumph; well-earned perspiration glistening from his forehead.

"You were wonderful!" gasped Milly afterwards. "Absolutely wonderful! It was like the old days!"

"It was rather enjoyable," Henry agreed.

## *Icarus In Reverse*

"And Mr. Simpkins says the switchboard's been jammed with heaps of praise. 'Never had so much weather in me life', one listener said. 'Keep it up. It's jolly good.'"

"I had no idea the weather could be so popular," replied Henry. "I thought people only wanted the likes of Brian le Saux".

"No," said Milly, who had once suffered badly at the hands of an E.P.Dawkins fitted toilet. "It's *real* weather they want. Honest weather. Not a cabaret. Real, reliable, radio weather!"

"Milly, that's marvellous!" exclaimed Henry. "Can I quote you on that?"

"Quote me on what, dear?"

"Your perfect assonance. Or is it alliteration?"

"There's no need to be vulgar, Mister Henry."

"No, Milly. It's just the apt juxtaposition of those wise words."

"I see." Milly was unconvinced.

"Real reliable weather," marvelled Henry. "It's perfect."

It was only later in the day when Henry overheard two of the presenters and the host of the afternoon show 'In the Potting Shed' comparing notes.

"It's very strange," said the first voice, whom he knew to be Roger's. "My script for programmes later on Radio Vivant seemed to have gone AWOL."

"Mine, too," said Denise.

Hubert Hubris, afternoon host for 'In the Potting Shed' agreed. "It was nowhere to be seen," he commiserated. "Instead, some daft pudding had chucked a Mission Statement on top of all my notes."

"I rather like Mission Statements," said Denise.

"But not at the expense of one's notes," commented Roger.

"No."

"How could it have happened?"

"General oversight, I suppose. Things will need to shape up within the department."

As Henry was summoned into Melchior Baldwin's office around five o'clock, he feared the worst. A savage carpeting, a punch-drunk bollocking awaited him, he was sure. Instead Melchior greeted him with an eerie smile and an enthusiastic arm gesture.

"Henry, I'll come straight to the point."

After seven or eight minutes, he eventually did.

"To sum up," he announced, as Henry was gazing distractedly out of the window, "we've had so many calls in praise of today's suddenly extended weather bulletin that we've decided to continue with the experiment for another month."

"Experiment? Another month?"

"Yes. A full three minute broadcast. It's what our public wants. It means more work for you, of course, but there we are. We must be *seen* to be listening to our listeners. So run along there. We must prepare for change!"

In a state of delirium, Henry raised himself languorously from the chair. How had it happened indeed? As he noticed the forlorn state of Melchior's variegated Tradescantia, an image suddenly imprinted itself upon him. Part of it was Milly's innocent tea-trolley weaving its way round the department, removing gratuitous advertising prompts and reminders under cover of the conveniently devious and distracting pink Mission Statement. The other was the same Milly singing harmoniously and sweetly now from a large fleecy Cumulus Nimbus cloud.

It was an inspiring image, he thought, and one to which he was profoundly and unreservedly grateful.

# The Clarity of Dialogue

She hadn't expected two of them! Perhaps he travelled with his secretary on home visits to save time. Laura was showing them into the sitting room where they took up opposite ends of the sofa.

"Can I get you anything? Something to drink, perhaps?"

"A glass of water, please," replied the woman tentatively. "If that's no trouble."

"We've got plenty of that," Laura smiled, but they failed to respond to her observation, sitting passively like a set of bookends or stone lions on duty outside a suburban garden gate.

She ran the tap for a second, casting a backward glance into the living room. There was a momentary rattling of paper, no doubt preparing the documents for the pension plan.

"Here you are," she said, passing the glass to the secretary.

"Thank you," the woman said, resting the glass on the nearby table.

Then, almost as one, they both asked, "And what do you think about the state of the world today?"

Laura hadn't expected a question like this, moments before they were going to conjecture on the current position of her savings.

"Well, I don't know," she began. "I think they've made it very difficult, haven't they?"

"For whom?"

"For savers, for instance."

"You mean the ministers?"

"Well no, I wasn't thinking of government particularly, but yes, I suppose so, yes. It all started with those banks!"

The woman threw her a non-sequitur with some reference at the end. Unless Laura was much mistaken, the woman said something about Corinthians. Clearly a Greek bank, then. She sat down opposite the two of them.

"It's very good of you to welcome us into your home," said the man.

"Well we could hardly do it outside in the rain," Laura replied.

Again there was the slightly puzzled look. The man was gazing back at her and she noticed the faint grey colour of his eyes. He appeared younger than she'd expected.

"*Some* people don't. In fact, a majority of them slam the door on us."

"But that seems a strange thing to do if they've made an appointment," commiserated Laura.

The two exchanged glances.

"You were *expecting* us?"

"Well, yes of course. Three thirty, they said."

The man was putting something into his briefcase.

"I'm Malcolm," he said. "And this is Cynthia."

"But *you're* the adviser?" Laura asked.

"We work in tandem. As a team." Malcolm smiled.

"We're *both* advisers," Cynthia beamed.

"It's just that I wasn't expecting two of you."

"We *always* work in twos," Cynthia affirmed.

"I suppose it's easier for taking notes," replied Laura.

"But why would we do that?" asked Malcolm. "Nothing is written down. We prefer the clarity and lucidity of dialogue."

It was when he said the last few words that Laura thought he was much too attractive to be a Pensions Adviser. They usually looked rather washed out like dishevelled car salesmen with a whiff of alcohol on their breath.

I like that, she thought to herself. 'The clarity of dialogue.' The direct approach was certainly preferable to those ghastly call centres where they asked you impertinent personal questions and claimed it was because of data protection.

"What about my contributions?" she asked them.

"You mean hospitality?" said Cynthia.

"I beg your pardon!"

"Well you've been *most* accommodating," observed Malcolm.

"I have?"

"Not everyone would admit us and give out glasses of water," confirmed Cynthia.

Laura felt suddenly very sorry for them. They must have had some appalling customers in the past. Ones that even slammed doors on them after having especially requested their personal services! It was a mixed-up, muddled-up, shook-up world, she thought, subsequently thinking of a song from nowhere in particular.

"I suppose no one likes form-filling," she commiserated. "Come to think of it, I'm not so keen on it myself."

"There *are* no forms to fill in," Malcolm assured her. "We're not like the Scientology people who give you a personality test."

"The Scientology people?"

"That's right. They're always very keen on recruiting."

"Recruiting?"

"Yes. And ten per cent donations. It's quite a tidy sum!"

"Ten per cent is quite good," Laura replied. "What with interest rates being so low at the moment."

"It depends on your earnings," said Cynthia.

"Well, I suppose it *would* do. Mind you, I only work part-time."

"Ah yes," said Malcolm. "We all serve in different ways."

"I see," Laura replied. She clearly didn't. "I mean is there anything else you can give me? If you say there are no forms."

"Well yes," said Malcolm, opening his briefcase. There is. Perhaps you'd like to read this at your leisure and we can come back and discuss it with you."

"I see," said Laura, but she was still none the wiser. "A preparation, perhaps?"

Cynthia was nodding enthusiastically. "We can always call back. Same time next week suit you?"

"Er well, yes."Laura replied. "If you're sure it's no trouble."

"It's no trouble in the slightest," cooed Cynthia softly. "Is it, Malcolm?"

Laura was seeing them out and together they tripped sedately down the garden path. They waved back at her as she closed the door. She picked up Malcolm's booklet. It was soft and flimsy to the touch and had a picture of a rising sun on it. It was no doubt a reference to Japan or one of the other emerging Tiger Economies. And then just below in large capitals was the word 'Watchtower.' Obviously a mention of the Ombudsman or was it maybe Watchdog? However, as she flipped through its floppy pages she could find no connection with pensions. They clearly wanted customers to perform a large amount of background reading.

The rest of the week ambled by. It was the onset of the blackcurrant season and she found herself crouching for long periods in front of heavily truss-laden shrubs. Pounds and pounds of sticky, glossy fruit perspired in panniers waiting to be turned into crumbles, coulis, jams, jellies, compotes, mousses and even cordials and wines. All but the last item was to make its way to the plethora of church bazaars and garden fetes that festooned the month of July. When Laura closed her eyes at night, she could see branches of blackcurrants waving in the summer breeze. At times the bushes almost seemed to sink to the ground, struggling to stay upright under the heavy burden of fruit.

It was one afternoon when heavily daubed in woad-like substances that she heard a knock at the door. The silhouette behind the frosted glass suggested a woman, maybe Mary Crabtree from the W.I. The visit was perhaps to chide her for her meagre output, but when she opened the door, mentally preparing herself for the forthcoming inevitable rebuke, she saw that it was Cynthia from the Pension Bureau.

"We just called about the book," she enquired. "Just passing. Wondered if it was any help?"

Laura wiped the congealed blackcurrants from her fingers onto her apron.

"I'm really sorry," she began. "It's been so frantic. I've been up to my eyes in..."

"Oh yes," said Cynthia, slightly put out. "But no matter. I just happened to be in the neighbourhood. We can call on you again."

"We?"

"Myself and Malcolm."

"Ah yes. I'll get my diary." Laura hastened into the bathroom catching a glimpse in the mirror of the fruit-stained tribal warrior that glanced back. A few frantic swishes did little to alleviate the daub. If anything, it elongated the purple smudges in a strangely contemporary way. Next Wednesday was the only diary day which was unadorned with jottings.

"Come for tea," she suggested.

"We will," said Cynthia, suddenly pleased.

"Four o'clock?"

"Make it three thirty. It'll give more time to chat."

Cynthia scuttled down the path, her faltering steps reminiscent of a TV comedian who often used the catchphrase 'awful.' Now how did it go? She could picture the tottering high heels but not the words. Closing the door on Cynthia, Laura settled down to more jam-making. The kitchen was awash with the tang of currants while her hair was sticky with the aroma of their leaves.

On the Wednesday morning, Laura made an alarming discovery. Sifting through the various shelves of the pantry, she suddenly realised she was out of tea. And tea was what they were invited for even though the last time Cynthia had only drunk water.

She hurried off into town, turning her back resolutely on the seductive duplicity of the supermarket with its various temptations. You always came out with more than you wanted – didn't actually need – and as for those girls at the till, they ranged from taciturn to comatose.

As she glanced up and down the street considering alternatives, she gazed with interest at a new establishment on the corner. Bold letters proclaimed 'Yin Ho – Chinese Eat and Delicacy.' Something wanted to make her go inside and correct Mr Ho's sentence. After all, shaky grammar was no advertisement for a new undertaking.

When the bell eventually stopped tinkling over the shop door, a man with an impassive face and white apron popped out from under the counter.

"I should be of assistance," he announced.

A marked contrast to the supermarket, she thought. 'Should be but can't be arsed.'

Mr Ho was looking at her strangely and she wondered if the inescapable blackcurrant was still in evidence.

"I have visitors," she began. "And a decision awaits my future for the time when I want to put my feet up."

Mr Yin Ho appeared puzzled. He stared at her purple fingernails.

"I think I need some tea. To mark the occasion."

"Ah yes," said Mr Ho. "You want *special* tea."

"Well, it might be nice," said Laura.

"Special tea is my speciality," he laughed, highly pleased at what might have been a first pun in English.

"Yes," said Laura, largely ignoring it and concentrating on the mission in hand. "They'll be tired with their trudging round all day so something to..."

"Raise their spirits?" enquired Mr Yin Ho softly. He pointed to a jar on the bottom shelf. "This one always good. My customers swear at it."

'By', she thought. It should be 'by', but she was far too polite to correct him.

"How much?" Mr Yin Ho asked.

"Just a quarter," Laura replied.

On the return journey she wondered why the packet was so large and the contents of Mr Yin's jar so greatly depleted. It was only when she passed the library, so often a trigger to understanding, that she realised he had emptied a quarter of the entire jar. She had been taken aback by the price too but having spent so much of the time in earnest conversation with Mr Yin Ho, she felt it would have been impolite to leave the shop empty-handed.

The contents agreeably perfumed the insides of her shopping bag, so often a sanctuary for escaped sweets which attempted to disguise themselves with fluff. It exuded a distinctive waft into her cupboard too. What must it taste like? All so often these products were less impressive than their enticing smells. She thought of Mr Yin Ho working alone in his shop and how he, on seeing his only customer perhaps for the day, had greeted her as a long-lost friend.

She bought extra milk and managed to find three cups without a chip. It was no good entrusting things to the dishwasher. Its boisterous nocturnal bumping, which she often heard from the bedroom, wreaked a calculated revenge on selected china. And it was lousy too at removing dried beetroot.

After three o'clock that afternoon, Laura kept casting an anxious eye from the upstairs window. Secreted behind a piece of net curtain, which looked as if it might have been one of

Salome's veils, she gazed at the unrevealing street. The pair of knickers that had spent several weeks in the lime tree had finally been rescued, thereby putting an end to speculation over their inclusion. Over to the left, Mrs Gigg's whirly-line had been taken down for the summer...

Her ruminating was suddenly interrupted by a perfunctory tap on the door. Two silhouettes appeared behind the pane of glass, reminiscent of a building society that had gone wrong or bust or been taken over or all three.

The door swung open revealing Malcolm and Cynthia in expectant eagerness.

"Ah yes," said Laura. "Please come in."

As they ventured in apprehensive tandem towards the living room, Laura noticed the pertness of Malcolm's buttocks within those unpromising grey flannels. They both sat upright in the same seats as before.

"I'll make the tea," Laura announced.

"Don't go to any trouble," suggested Malcolm.

"It's no trouble," said Laura. "It's Chinese."

As Malcolm and Cynthia sat in meditative silence, they could hear the sounds of cups and saucers clinking in the kitchen. Laura eventually emerged triumphant holding a tray of tea-cups, pot and biscuits.

"I bought some Fortune Cookies," she smiled. "My friend Dorothy says they're rather bland but the biscuits themselves offer some interesting interpretations."

She poured the tea, unleashing its aroma on the sitting room.

"Smells nice," said Cynthia.

"Got it in special," beamed Laura.

The sunlight was filtering through the living room window, its shafts of golden radiance making Malcolm appear like some latter-day saint. They sipped their tea in silence, listening to the occasional coo of a pigeon from the patio. Laura felt the tea catch the back of her throat suddenly.

"Bit different," she choked, but her visitors were still coming to terms with the taste.

"Fruity!"

"Did you get time?" Cynthia queried. "You know, with the reading?"

"Ah yes," said Laura. "To be honest, I haven't really had a moment."

Cynthia's cheerful demeanour altered a fraction. For a moment Laura detected a slight tinge of impatience.

"I've been quite busy, what with one thing and another. I haven't had a chance to read your chronicle. Investments, wasn't it?"

Cynthia had relinquished her tea. For a second Laura caught sight of how flushed they suddenly both looked. She patted her own cheeks, noticing that they too were a little moist.

I'd rather be patting Malcolm's cheeks, she thought, and giggled at the prospect.

"Something funny?" Cynthia enquired. "From our point of view it's rather remiss that you haven't given yourself time to…"

Malcolm seemed about to interrupt her.

"Our publication provides plentiful food for thought and substance for debate."

"I'm so sorry," replied Laura, thinking that Cynthia looked like a cross between a maiden aunt and an off-duty librarian.

"It's all right, Cynthia," Malcolm soothed. "We can take up the discussion from here. It's not always possible to make adequate preparation."

Definitely, thought Laura, admiring Malcolm's sudden assertiveness.

"Another tea?"

They both nodded.

Malcolm's eyes were growing lighter now in the pale sunlight while Cynthia mercifully seemed to sink back into the shadows. Laura's gaze drifted back to Malcolm. He appeared younger, flanked as he was by the sombre furniture of the room.

"The Watchtower," Malcolm began.

"Oh yes," said Laura. "I can't always find my glasses."

It sounded like a lame excuse and Cynthia was still looking at her somewhat sourly.

Tower, she thought to herself. Tower. She had once read the Master Builder by Henrik Ibsen and was astonished to find that the tower symbolised orgasm. She glanced back at Malcolm, noticing that the hairs on his chest were attempting to escape from within his shirt. Another sip of the tea and the room took on a surprisingly mellow glow.

"I'm so sorry I didn't read your magazine," she confessed. "You would be quite within your rights to spank me. And you *are* so very attractive!"

Where had the words come from? What was happening? Laura took a fugitive sip of tea but that only made matters worse.

"You're quite nice, too," responded Malcolm. "In fact, I've been looking forward to our visit all week."

"Oh," said Laura.

Cynthia seemed to have melted away into the background.

"Perhaps we could go somewhere more comfortable?" suggested Malcolm.

Laura already sensed the beckoning image of the bedroom.

"But what about Cynthia?" she asked. "Won't it be a little...?"

"I'm quite happy to come along too," Cynthia blurted. Her cheeks were rosy-hued, her aspect altogether less librarian. "We usually do these things in tandem."

*Icarus In Reverse*

Not the bedroom, surely, thought Laura, but she shrugged it off as the three of them quickly ascended the staircase.

In the frantic flurry of clothes-discarding, an image suddenly imprinted itself on Laura.

It was the calm face of Mr Yin Ho, pouring out the generous quarter, packaging it, handing it to her with a knowing yet inscrutable expression.

# A Dash of Soda

Hello. I am a big girl with what you might describe as a Renoir-like body.
No. That won't do. I'll start again.
Let's begin with introductions. I'm Laura Cleo Cuthbert. L.C.C as one of my cousins used to say. Apparently I reminded him of a cricket club. Another said my names made him think of a hermaphrodite. These are some of the things I have to live with!

They do say that when you meet someone for the first time you should say their name back to them within thirty seconds, otherwise it's gone forever. So just in case you've forgotten, the name's Laura. L.C.C.

I was talking about my husband, the first man I knew in the biblical sense of the word, or about to. I expect you might be wondering where we met. People often do. A cinema, a party or a dance hall perhaps? No, it was none of them. I met him in the street outside number forty two, Athelstan Road.

I often wonder who devises the street names. Whether there's a book they use or a committee.

He was bending over a bicycle, repairing it almost tenderly. I was attracted to the neat curve of his back and the light blue flannel trousers. His hands seemed to be getting liberally covered with oil and he raised an arm to brush away something that had landed on his cheek. Sandy auburn hair was suddenly lit up in a momentary burst of sun.

I kept looking studiously and then glancing away in case someone spotted me.

## Icarus In Reverse

I pretended I was waiting for a bus – only there was no stop – or waiting for someone, gazing up in fake expectation, marvelling at those tight curves in those fortunate blue flannels.

The repair took quite a few minutes but I was nowhere near sated. Eventually I stole reluctantly away before he could turn round and spot his silent admirer.

When I closed my eyes later that evening the image of the attended bicycle remained firmly in my mind, the moment of the illuminating sun like an usherette shining a torch into a darkened picture palace.

And now I knew where he lived, most probably. I earmarked the house and then made a point of strolling past it three or four times a day. The repair, however, had clearly been effective as I no longer saw him in the street and instead gazed up at the pale blank windows for any sign of life.

The summer was a long barren period. The routine walks proved fruitless. I often wished I had a dog; an excuse on a lead and so often an easy way of entering into conversation. I was on holiday now and so was he probably.

Autumn came. Large leaves cascading from plane trees with peeling bark.

And then one day, as I walked past the door, it unexpectedly opened. I could see the tell-tale blue flannelled legs approaching. I cast my eyes down, anxious not to appear too keen and took a slightly quicker stride as if on a purposeful mission. Suddenly I felt my front leg slip and slide. I capsized, virtually doing the splits. I had been brought down by a soggy plane leaf.

He was attentive, helping me up.

"Are you all right?" he enquired.

"Yes, yes," I gasped, realising his helping hands had violently increased my breath intake.

"That's all right, then," he said and gently relinquished my arm.

I realised then that I had to seize the moment, exploit this foible of fate.

"Do you mind if I sit on your wall?" I panted. "Just for a minute?"

At least I hadn't said something like 'knee' and subsequently betrayed myself.

"Feel free," he said, gesturing to the wall.

I sat there recuperating with my attendant onlooker.

"Would you like a cup of tea?" he offered at length.

He no doubt realised that tea was beneficial in cases of shock, whereas in old movies they miraculously pull out brandy flasks from nowhere. I would have taken anything. Paraffin! Syrup of figs! Halibut oil!

I sat down calmly on the wall, *his* wall, feeling the brickwork sink in and chafe my buttocks. As I said, I was large then, and am so now, but I was not always so, not this strongly built – not 'in between'.

I sat there while he was making the tea, visualising his small kitchen and softly singing kettle, when all of a sudden two bricks fell alarmingly away from the wall. I got up immediately, remembering at the same time my old grandfather's adage about buttocks, cold stones and 'piles'.

I was also worried that a suddenly collapsed wall might taint my dramatic arrival.

Quickly I wandered into the house, away from the scene of the damage and stepped into *his* world. The tea he offered me was both weak and sweet. His parents were busy at work, he said. His brother too. There was a photo of both of them on the sideboard. They were not dissimilar to each other.

"Your brother?" I enquired.

He nodded. "Phil." Then. "I'm Gary," he said, pointing to himself.

"Laura," I reciprocated and cooed slightly.

When I went later in the week to plant a thank you note through the door, I noticed the brickwork of the garden wall had been repaired. As I placed the letter into the gaping aperture, struggling momentarily with the bristles that guarded the letterbox, someone spotted me through the front room window. He immediately flung open the door and I half expected a rebuke about the wall.

"A note" I said, indicating the profoundly obvious.

"Come on in," he invited.

This time the tea was consumed inside the house, where I could do less damage.

"Unless you'd like something stronger?" he offered.

"Only you," I nearly said and sweetly simpered instead.

We got talking. He asked me out. An Italian restaurant in the High Street with an absurdly large, phallic pepper dispenser. It got me thinking.

We began to see each other regularly. At weekends I cooked meals for him in our small flat. I was amazed at the volume he could put away. Occasionally I would tease him, make references to a sea bird that rhymed with Thanet, and we would mock fight as he grabbed my flailing wrists.

I noticed that when we wrestled, albeit briefly, a ruler-like protrusion would appear within his trousers. It would last all through dinner and beyond...

After a meal one evening with avocado and celery, seafood platter with liberal sprinklings of oysters, washed down with 'pomegranate supreme' for afters, I let dinner take its course along with a bottle of lightly carbonated Rose.

"Let's..." I began and lunged towards the settee.

To my frustration he played the gentleman!

"Is it sex before marriage?" I queried, offering an explanation.

I had indirectly proposed!

"Yes," he slurred slightly.

I wondered if he was a covert Roman Catholic although there were no signs inside the house.

We got married the following autumn. I gazed at the leafless plane trees and expressed my untold gratitude. I was even more thankful for the absence of the obligatory disco. There was a barn-dance instead of greater complexity. When I noticed the ruler-like elevation that inhabited his dancing trousers my mouth went dry and hoarse in expectation.

That evening in the hotel he hurled his clothes onto the settee and took me in his arms. Delicacy forbids further detail. I take it you've been there yourself.

Yet oddly enough I felt disappointed – not with Gary who reared like a stallion – but with my own capacity for enjoyment. We went at it most nights, usually after the Ten O'Clock News and just before Book at Bedtime. Gary sang like a nocturnal owl but I'm afraid I contributed very little to the proceedings. He didn't seem to mind. He usually rolled over and fell asleep, sometimes imitating those steam trains that he was so fond of.

One day I went into work after a particularly steamy night and was met by a highly tearful Eunice.

"They're cutting our hours," she quivered.

The bakery was currently experiencing a downturn. Customers had been seen in the new hypermarket!

As I now finished work just before midday I decided to take on a bar job at Ye Olde Red Lion. It was one of those mysterious places; very dark, dull faint muzak on, which was always the same. Presumably no one could see the switch to turn it off.

Occasionally Gary would pop in to see me. Between clients very often. Did I tell you he was a carpenter? Freelance.

One morning the bar was oddly deserted and I was wading around in the gloom in my rather prim uniform when Gary came in. Unusually he accepted a drink.

"No one for this afternoon?" I asked.

"Mrs Haddiscoe," he announced to the empty space. "Cancelled again."

## Icarus In Reverse

He was sipping Pickled Henry's Old Cyder which sat in a small barrel on the bar.

"You haven't got the car?" I asked anxiously.

"Of course not. Came on me bike."

It was still the same bike as at the start of the story. I felt a momentary romantic glow.

"What'll you do later?"

He was on his second Pickled Henry.

"I don't know," he announced, his voice gradually becoming louder. "Go back home. Have a wank, I suppose."

I stood frozen at the serving hatch wondering if any customers were secreted in the gloomy alcoves. And then – I don't know – my arms reached out for an object perching innocently on the bar. I raised it up and squeezed it, sending a large jet of soda stream towards Gary. He shook like a stunned dog that has been tapped on the nose. He gasped, shook off the droplets and I squirted again.

There was a flicker of anger within his normally mild features. Suddenly he grabbed me from behind the hatch, yanked me over a bar stool and lifted up my Cook and Brewer apron.

What followed was entirely unexpected.

I was subjected to a retaliatory spanking and then – from nowhere it seemed –

I experienced a sudden orgasm of bewildering intensity! We rolled about on the Red Lion carpet, two owls hooting in the light of day.

I don't know whether Gary's exposed and classical buttocks were spotted by a passer-by but my probationary period was never extended. Again the hypermarket was conveniently blamed for the decline in trade.

But now the pattern was set. Gary would spank me before the evening soap, sometimes during the adverts, and then again afterwards. There was also our traditional slot before Book at Bedtime. I was overwhelmed. I couldn't get enough. I was deeply glad that he was a carpenter by profession.

Sometimes, if he had a splinter, he would use the additional support of a table-tennis bat, which I had bought him for his birthday. I was in my element now and sometimes adopted the persona of 'Sylvie the Maid' who had forgotten to remove stray socks and pillow cases from underneath the bed.

Then one day disaster struck.

Gary, who had been having problems with his tinnitus, failed to hear the soporific drone of George McCarthy's milk float. They rang me up while I was putting the finishing touches to a hotpot.

The voice was soft, reflective.

I put down the towel and thought of falling plane leaves.

So there we have it. I'm available again. On the market. Anxiously looking for a carpenter's touch, or anyone's come to think of it.

The name's Laura. L.C.C. And by the way, I have a soda siphon.

# Holy Orders

It was a fine soft day. The cathedral stuck its head out of the low-floating mists that drifted over marshlands to the east. Wafting out into the vast porch with stone plinths on either side was the heady smell of lilies. And Stella could smell incense. Letting her nostrils take in the aroma, she closed her eyes momentarily as though entering some brew-house of delights. Her tongue tantalisingly licked her lips as if to suggest she was posing for a photo. It was all going to be fine. A perfect day, the ideal setting.

It was some while since she'd first toyed with the idea. Her uncle Cyril had proclaimed that there would *never* be a woman on the altar in *his* lifetime! Then when it did happen, when it finally came to pass, he unexpectedly defected to the Roman Catholics. Cyril stuck it out bravely. The banjos, the half-hearted singing, the quivering hymns and lack of incense, and the need to tell you what was going on at each stage of the ceremony, as if you had stepped inside the portals for the first time.

Stella took a malevolent delight in the sufferings of Uncle Cyril. And now, to top it all, she was about to reap her own reward and ascend to the priestly throne. In fact, she was to be 'crowned', for it felt more like a coronation in such sumptuous surroundings – albeit built by Catholics but never used to proper effect by its righteous reformers. And she was to have a parish near the cathedral! A tiny congregation nestling in the village of Lower Wimple. And wasn't the village's name of some religious significance too? She pictured a silent nun floating past a village pond.

Of course, she would have to leave her post at Sidebrook University, the department she had run so...

She was distracted by adjectives as she entered the building. The magisterial wide aisle, the reverential shadows... The sun was throwing stained glass patterns onto pillars and they merged and blended into the shape of a crown. In five hours' time it would all have taken place; the organ breaking into jubilation, the white collar that was to decorate her pulsing and slightly apprehensive neck now a permanent fixture. If only Uncle Cyril could see her now! He would choke into his brown ale sending its heavy froth flying up onto his nose.

It was cool inside; remnants of a summer's day clearly banished and given over to reverential quiet. The tourists had not arrived yet, their protruding cameras inevitably slung across oval tummies, oddly phallic and telescope-like. But now even *they* used smaller devices – mobile phones, digital appliances...

She gazed at the Prior's Door whose intricate carving heralded a passage to nowhere. She tried to decipher the figures and animals which adorned each side, but it was too early to buy a guide which would have explained what lay in front of her. The bookshop closed, she drifted slowly round the rest of the building, her coat flapping gently and occasionally against the stonework. Only when she crossed one of the transepts did a stone carving suddenly catch her eye. It was one of the few remaining statues; one that had escaped the belligerence of Henry's followers and the indignant piety of Puritans.

Stella moved away but the statue's gaze seemed to follow her. Pity, she thought to herself, that they had missed this one and yet broken the others. There could have been a better swap. She gazed up and again found herself caught in the beam of the image's eye. If anything it appeared more scowling, ever more disapproving. What had happened to serene medieval maidenly qualities that were more apposite in a building such as this? No, this sculpture was altogether more combative, truculent even, smirking malevolence downwards like an imp.

Stella stepped out into the bright sunlight of the dismantled cloisters of which only a few patterns remained on the brickwork. She decided to return to her room, do a little quiet liturgical reading and pour herself a coffee. The family was coming up at two; a motley flotilla that included the perpetually runny-nosed grandchildren. She hoped they wouldn't be a nuisance today, emitting gurgled coos and staccato yelps during the hushed and reverential moments of the ceremony. Linda would have to be *spoken* to and, if necessary be prepared to take Sasha and Toja out.

She particularly disliked Toja – not just the name, which sounded like some unpleasant kind of biting insect, but the grubby and dishevelled landscape of his face. The child was never clean, not since the time when he had first started leaving puddles in supermarkets. It was altogether too embarrassing. She had wanted to drown him in one after he had left a large lagoon near the frozen fish counter. A squadron of staff had been quickly mobilised with mops.

Sitting now in the soft silence of her small hotel she noticed a last coffee sachet lingering on the poppy-flowered tea tray. The kettle hummed obligingly and she poured its steaming contents over the dark-smelling granules which had a peculiar odour of armpits. After a few minutes she took the cup to her lips and drank deeply.

"Please," said Polly Teague. "It would be very helpful if..."

Stella Studgate looked up. "I can't change your hours. Couldn't possibly. Have no room for manoeuvre."

There were certain phrases she liked, those that she had an affinity with, and this was one of them. She was also quite partial to the phrases that her obliging cohort Greyhope Wortle was apt to quote. His was an impressive collection of 'respect, challenging and transparent', and, of course, the 'learning experience.' One day he came out with all of them in a single sentence. She was intoxicated with wonder and sensed him purring inwardly in delight and self-belief.

"But my sister's getting worse," pleaded Polly.

Stella was becoming annoyed. Polly had her earnest and slightly aggrieved face on.

"If you *wish* to change your hours," Stella asserted, "then you will have to *resign* your current ones and apply for the hours you seek at interview."

"Interview? But can't I just swap with Tom Lush. He has *day* classes not evenings. Besides, he's got a car."

"His vehicular arrangements are of no concern of mine," Stella replied imperiously. Greyhope would have liked that one.

"He doesn't have a disability either," continued Polly, annoyed now that she had to resort to the 'D' word.

Stella Studgate gazed back impassively.

"Resign and reapply!" she repeated, her massive form heaving ominously from behind the desk.

Polly sidled out of the office. She was turning into a nuisance, Stella thought, and made a note to reduce some of her hours the following term. The numbers often dwindled in the spring and it would be an apt reprisal for uttering that dirty 'D' word! There would be no opposition from Polly now.

Suddenly there was an almighty crash in the corridor and a tinkling of china cups. Polly had reversed sideways and collided with Sabina Shudmire's tea trolley. Stella shut the door on her in disgust. She left them to the sounds of spoons and confusion as the 'interview' was now successfully concluded. 'Change her hours indeed!' Well, it was out of the question and she had astutely fobbed off Polly with what she thought was a highly ingenious managerial device. It was so much nicer to have unobtrusive staff, ones that asked no questions at all or queried the impeccable structure of the teaching roster. Stella emerged triumphantly from her desk, her vast bottom swinging from side to side like a rhino's or a large Aberdeen Angus.

Placing her cup under the fickle hot water machine which gurgled and emitted a few exuberant bubbles, she could hear Polly's distraught sobs down the corridor. Polly should know better than to be difficult. Why couldn't they accept what had been so carefully prescribed for the last ten years? Why rock the boat with alteration? The last thing the department wanted was untidy swaps which would disturb the smooth running of the timetable.

Stella's time honoured motto was to introduce changes that she herself liked and then consult. It was, after all, the tried and tested Sidebrook way. Staff of greater experience, of more meditative and congenial wisdom, knew better than to ruffle the waters, opting instead for the sweet stink of unchallenged stagnation.

Polly was so unlike Greyhope, who ever since he had arrived had adopted a sapient strategy of obsequiousness. He was, moreover, a model spy, his quiet and unassuming manner enabling him to pick up voices of dissent and relate them assiduously back to Stella, whereupon they would be suitably purged. He had done no different at school, his talent for informing on the mooning pupils of the cherry orchard earning him a special accolade. He became Head Prefect. From then on there was no looking back.

No, the department was a Cross Channel ferry, cheerfully heaving in one direction only and determinedly resolved not to flounder on the choppy seas of consensus.

Stella took her robe out of the wardrobe. She had been longing to wear it all morning and now the urge was too great. She emerged from the room like a giant ink blob, her rippling and bovine buttocks elegantly concealed by the dark fabric of the cassock. For hours she had pondered over the priestly catalogue, opting for a tasteful if slightly grainy shade of charcoal. Placing her luggage quickly in the ample Volvo she headed silently towards the cathedral.

The organ was playing a classical rendition of 'Raindrops Keep Falling on My Head' as she entered the nave. From somewhere she heard the steely chink of a censer, as a wafting puff of incense drifted across the vaulted ceiling. The organ had forsaken 'Raindrops' now and with an imperial swirl announced Stella's approach towards her allotted place. Rows of darkly costumed men turned to look at her. She smiled gracefully and took up her seat.

Suddenly something made her look up and she found she was sitting under the repulsive statue she had seen earlier.

"What *is* that?" she asked a colleague anxiously.

"It's the bishop, dear," said the elderly priest who had just woken up.

"No, no," Stella continued. "That awful image here." She jerked a finger upwards which was nearly taken amiss by a row of clergy opposite.

"Ah, that is Saint Catherine the Less of Ponders End. I venture to say she only looks that way because part of her cheek is missing. Oh and there's the top of her ear, too."

Stella tried to look away but at various times during the service Saint Catherine returned to stare at her and haunt her. She was at her most threatening when they were giving the sign of peace as Stella deposited her enthusiastic paw into the over-appreciative hands of an elderly gent with huge sideburns.

Saint Catherine scowled fiercely at Stella's professed humility and suddenly, within that scowl, Stella recognised a

## Icarus In Reverse

familiar face. It was none other than Polly Teague. The same overhanging lip and querulous expression as witnessed when she had last asked Stella her vexatious questions. But now under the panoply of vaulted arches it was Polly Teague with a far more sinister and menacing eye.

Typical, thought Stella. Typical of her to spoil her big day, as she ran a tentative finger around her collar in the way a real vicar might have done – or even a lady vicar. Stella would try to acquire a more maidenly demeanour, a range of doey-eyed expressions of understanding.

Outside the bright sunlight made her squint as the various shades of clergy milled around before assembling for a final group photo.

"I expect you'd like to see your parish now," said a tall gentleman after the photograph had eventually been taken.

Stella was mildly taken aback. "Well, yes. Er, why not?"

As they drove over the undemanding bumps of countryside they could see the slightly lopsided tower of Lower Wimple. A little group had formed outside the church, a posse of flower ladies or cleaners. Eagerly they welcomed their new vicar and escorted her through the porch.

"It's *so* nice to meet you," Stella beamed.

"Likewise," echoed the ladies.

As Stella walked with them up towards the chancel she suddenly glanced up.

"What on earth is *that?*" she found herself asking in alarm and pointed with a nervously trembling finger.

A face she had seen earlier stared back at her.

"Why, Saint Catherine," they all chimed gaily. "Saint Catherine of Ponders End. The church is, after all, dedicated to her!"

The odious Polly Teague glowered back at her, a face of cold, haughty and truculent disdain.

"We'll see about that," Stella muttered beneath clenched teeth. "Oh yes!"

And already in her mind's eye she was drawing up plans for a sudden and unexpected removal.

*Dominic O'Sullivan*

# Without Eaves

They had cancelled the train I was due to take, the indicator displaying the solitary word on a dark, unhelpful board. There was no explanation other than the destination, situated at the end of an off-shoot line, was probably less favoured, less popular away from the main commuter track, so frankly why bother?

I didn't relish another hour in a frenetic mainline station littered with brightly-lit shops and rancid coffee bars so I stole, probably illicitly, onto a Norwich train. They kept announcing about eligible tickets for travel, which, along with the peculiar intricacies of off-peak railcards, meant that I very likely couldn't. I sat quietly thereafter waiting for a possible inquisition whereupon I would point to the mysteriously cancelled train and stress the urgent nature of my journey.

The train was relatively full but there was still room and I sat with an empty seat beside me. The girders of the terminus withdrew eventually; we were sidling along high black walls, the site of the old Bishopsgate station, I'm told. Speed was a contemplative affair; it wasn't until Stratford that the train revved up to a more acceptable rhythm. No doubt they wanted us to gaze upon the Olympic glories of a rejuvenated Stratford but at the last minute I forgot to glance out and saw only the red and blue of a Central Line train heading along a platform. That was when I first became aware.

"Julia," snapped a voice behind me. "Julia."
Julia, wherever she was, was clearly not responding.

## Icarus In Reverse

"Ah, Julia," said the speaker again. "Look, I've had a problem with KBN and they want to change tomorrow."

A pause.

"I know it's rather annoying really. I was wondering if you could look at the dates and tell me when we can reschedule."

The realisation, unwelcome when it came, that I was now captive to a monologue of office proportions.

"Julia?"

She had obviously gone again or was spreading out the diary, gazing at a screen, figuring out the speaker's movements. Julia, guardian of commitments, custodian of the schedule. She had given a reply. We were passing Goodmayes now, a name with its own puzzlement. Mayes?

"No, that's no good!" he barked. "They should know that!"

A patch of green appeared briefly – a hint of things to come.

"Yeah," said a voice to my left, confidentially. "It's me."

I wondered if this was some kind of introduction, but then I saw the cell-phone clasped to his ear, as if he was listening to the sea in a shell. A can of beer was clutched in the other hand.

"Yeah, babes. I managed to talk to him."

"Julia!"

"Depends when he's free."

"I couldn't possibly do that!"

I wanted to say one at a time, please, gentlemen, to mediate, but of course you can't. Each, by virtue of the conversation, was blissfully unaware of the other, whereas I...

The train was slowing down, the conversations sharper, more animated. The second speaker was dialling again and I hoped in vain for a tunnel with its welcome blast of frigid air, where suddenly an enveloping blackness cuts out all external contact...

My desire for a dark cavern made me think of a tale I had once read, coincidentally on a train, where the seasoned traveller knows the *exact* duration of a particular tunnel on his journey. At a given point the landscape would subside into a string of cables, long languid dipping wires bobbing up and down like mesmeric waves against the darkness. Hypnotic under closer inspection, like snakes unfurling their endless coils.

But then the tunnel goes on *beyond* the accepted point, the specified duration. It continues and confounds the expectations of the passenger. He tells a woman in the seat opposite that the tunnel should have ended two and a half minutes ago! She seems unconvinced, unconcerned. On and on the tunnel goes, cable after cable, the whole world converted into tunnel. At length, he finds a guard, tells him the computations, which, if he is a seasoned guard, he would already know. But the man in blue and grey doesn't care or seem to. On and on they travel, the tunnel ever lengthening, the cables becoming more obscure, mere pencil lines, subsumed now into frightening allegorical portents of...

"Look again!" he screams behind me.

I see Julia's office reduced to panic now, a state of confusion, the much sought after information multiplied into various misleading diaries, papers, folders, files, and the desk has now become a labyrinth.

"Yes, I'll have a word," he says on my left. "Hello."

And finally we hit a tunnel. We really do. But only of five or six seconds duration, not enough to change...

"Hello," he says again, the interruption over. "I'm on the train."

There's a pause while the information's being digested.

"Are you being a good boy?" he asks the other voice. "Helping?"

The phone is hissing, scratching, competing with the galloping train. And a sound like a muffled cough comes from

## Icarus In Reverse

the other end and I realise that for whoever's speaking an amplifier's been switched on. The beer can is lifted, raised, poured thoughtfully into expectant lips.

"Are you being good? 'Cos if not when I come home I'm gonna smack your bum."

Indeterminate sound, cacophony from the cell-phone. Whoever's on the line says nothing, acknowledging the beer-tinted threat.

"Oh for heaven's sake!"

Julia has probably ransacked the place or thrown her foot into a computer screen.

"Yeah, I'll be home later," mutters the threat. He clasps the beer can tighter. A woman's voice is now enquiring. The amplifier's still switched on.

And realising the phone is broadcasting out into the carriage he yells to her to turn it off.

"You what?"

"Turn it down!"

"Turn what down?"

A swig of beer and a snarl.

"The bloody amplifier, that's what!"

She's fumbling with something, staring at the dial.

"You stupid cow," he mutters softly.

"I can't cancel if I don't know what time!" screams the voice behind.

I think of my nullified train, eaten up into the ether, eternal like Duerrenmatt's Tunnel. It presses home the sense of loss.

And I see it sitting smugly in the sidings.

"Love you, babe," simpers the voice on my left. It takes another drink.

And I begin to wonder why the invisible boy had to use an amplifier. Why he needed it to hear. And suddenly, in the reflection of a passing train, I see a silent fist flying across his ear and he jettisons across the room.

My imagination's running away with me like this speeding train. It was the tunnel or lack of it; black salvation, things beyond our control.

And then I suddenly have a belated realisation, as if awakening from a torpor.

On the Wi-fi window and beyond lies a sign which indicates 'Quiet Zone'.

Here no mobile phones will reign, or shouldn't. There's a picture on the glass with a heavy line across. Gratefully, I stumble towards the door which hesitates and grudgingly allows me in. I gaze on the scene of soft serenity; the Quiet Zone with its promise of temporary calm, its offer of reasonable reassurance.

And I leave them both behind – the two worlds, that is, of largely suspected tyrannies.

*Icarus In Reverse*

# Kop Kun Krap

It was a relatively cool morning when Henry Wentworth stepped inside his greenhouse. He'd regretted placing it under the laburnum tree and now leaves had piled outside from last night's blustery storm. As he brushed past some plants on the left, there was a stale odour from their forlorn leaves – invariably so, but today it was more pronounced.

He picked up the secateurs and delicately dead-headed the offenders. On removing the spent leaves and blooms, he suddenly noticed a tiny bud behind them. It was the obdurate orchid, which so far had refused to flower. Henry stared at it for a moment in disbelief. For Henry this was often the most productive part of the day; those spare horticultural moments before he donned his coat and trudged up the road to work.

He had always enjoyed what he did – the various courses with the students – up until now, that is. Inexplicably, the establishment, the university for whom he had worked, had suddenly set up a 'partnership' with Sid Nuttall's property company. He remembered Sid droning on once at a meeting to which he surprisingly had been invited – and at whose request Henry couldn't recall – that 'the future lay in student accommodation'. Thereupon Sid's enterprises had immediately diversified and the odd-sounding UNIT had been created. From UNIT sprang a further subsidiary, ONTI.

It was not long before UNIT became known as 'Unbelievably Naff and Ineffectual Tuition', with Sid as its guiding light, whereas ONTI defied description. To make matters worse, they had been obliged to move out of their beautifully grandiose, quasi-Gothic building with its Byzantine twin towers and into one of Sid's new transparent erections. From the busy streets snaking below, staff and teaching rooms had become no longer private, thereby putting an end to a number of amorous trysts that had commenced in some of the classrooms. Neighbouring tall buildings blotted out sky and daylight alike so that everything seemed permanently cast in shadow. Quite appropriately, Henry thought, as if teaching had been subjected to a permanent eclipse, out-glossed only by presentation and show.

There was a touch of drizzle in the air, he noticed, as he set off to the nearby tube station. Plane trees with their peeling bark shed leaves onto the pavements. Beneath the trees, cardboard boxes and traces of discarded burger lurked, the polystyrene boxes that had once contained them now blown open to the elements.

The train was overcrowded so he had to stand. Very often it waited mysteriously between stations thereby adding to the travelling experience. At the next stop two tall oriental boys joined the train. Their overhanging armpits formed a canopy for Henry. They smiled as if apologising for disturbing him, for intruding onto treasured space. The train braked suddenly and Henry found himself in the armpit to the left.

"I'm so sorry," he murmured.

The taller of the two grinned and bowed. As Henry listened to the ensuing conversation he could hear a lot of 'kraps' being spoken and from his limited knowledge he decided they were Thai.

At the next station the train swelled further with passengers. The smiles and 'kraps' disappeared and were replaced by shapes in toothpaste-like suits; people who probably had connections with some of Sid Nuttall's various enterprises.

Henry staggered from the train at Liverpool Street. Here too was a maze of passing figures which he had to dodge both

## Icarus In Reverse

deftly and carefully. It was the elbows that were the most lethal, along with the rucksacks and shoulder-bags which lay in wait to jostle, bruise and bounce.

Arthur the doorman was more lugubrious than usual that morning.

"It's them bloody gates," he complained. "They keep beeping."

"I can't hear anything," replied Henry.

"Well they do," moaned Arthur. "They come and go."

Henry waved his card over the machine and the gates like predatory jaws swung open. He remembered the time when his friend Immelda, a lady of ample circumference, had got impaled on one of them.

"Here's me bust, me bottom's coming!" she announced in a northern accent.

But to no avail. The machines took no heed of the warning.

On the first floor Henry walked past the array of open doors. Director Supreme, Quentin Narsell, was at the end, strategically positioned to survey the comings and goings of the corridor. He had not been there for very long having moved from some position in the air force straight through to education.

I'm a high flyer," was his perennial and solitary joke.

Marjorie had called him Biggles but this still seemed too amiable for one who perpetuated the reign of terror that held sway over UNIT and its sidekick ONTI.

It was during lunch when Henry was unwrapping a perspiring cheese roll that had been entombed in cellophane for several weeks that he received a message from Bernie, one of his ex-students, who had returned to ONTI as a cleaner.

"Mr Arsehole want to see you."

Bernie had never seen the necessity to attach the letter 's' to verbs, which meant he had gone down very well in Norwich.

"Pardon, Bernie?" queried Henry, not sure which he should correct.

"Need to see you."

"You mean Mr Narsell?"

"Yes. Mr Arsehole."

If only pronunciation had been given a higher profile, he thought, instead of countless, meaningless tests.

'Pronunciation is the window of your linguistic knowledge' he had inscribed on more than one whiteboard, but to little effect. Mind you, perhaps Bernie had a point.

"You're sure it's *him*?"

"Yes. Mr Biggles."

Bernie had spent time with Marjorie too, who had a hankering after men with large feet, and one evening he had cooked her a Thai curry.

"Thank you, Bernie," said Henry.

Bernie had quickly abandoned his Thai name when he arrived on the grounds that it contained too many letters for the forms that ONTI was so fond of. Some of his fellow country-folk were even more economical and had reduced their names to single letters. He had had a B in one class and an O and possibly a ...

He strolled meditatively towards the suggested chamber with the perennially open door but the newly renamed Director of Operations was nowhere to be seen.

Resuming his seat in the vastly overcrowded staffroom, which he often referred to as the cattle byre, he saw a post-it note stuck to his telephone confirming the summons. He would go back later as Biggles was clearly flying some reconnaissance mission where he would observe for himself the activities of the industrious teaching staff, now relegated to the roles of office workers and whose weird contracts necessitated a punitive confinement from 8.30 till 5. The logic had always escaped him, though he suspected that Sid had always disliked teachers.

## Icarus In Reverse

Suddenly the phone rang. Biggles purred at the other end. "I'm available," he said.

He sounded like a cheap tart.

"Yes," replied Henry.

Quentin's door was open; a dimly-lit room with a little off-shoot where a low coffee table lurked. This was for 'cosy' chats.

"Come in," invited Squadron-Leader Biggles. Or was it Captain?

He moved towards Henry with a gesturing hand and shut the door behind him. This seemed ominous Henry thought.

"I just thought I'd have a quick word about results. Okay?"

Oh yes, thought Henry. The now departed summer course, vanished like a farting swallow. When the University had run it, it had gone by the slightly unglamorous name of 'The Pre-Sessional', but one of Biggles' crowning achievements was to rechristen it. Now revamped and revitalised it was known as the Rapid Foundation Induction.

"Rather a lot of failures," grumbled Quentin.

Henry was trying to recall the number of students that could actually string sentences together. He got halfway through to the second hand.

"They *were* quite weak," he advised him.

"Maybe," conceded Quentin. "But the university to whom we are partnered has complained of a dramatic loss of income."

"But they couldn't speak!" protested Henry.

"It's not important," retorted Quentin.

"Well what are they supposed to do, then? What are *we* supposed to do?"

"Adjust our quotas," continued Quentin.

Was he talking butter or grain?

"No more than three per cent failure rate. That way everybody's happy. Us, the students, the university. I can see it now." His eyes lit up. "A pass rate of ninety seven per cent! We can put that on the brochure too."

I suppose they could all graduate and become cleaners thought Henry. But no. And what did it mean anyway? His local railway boasted charts of ninety seven and ninety eight percent but he had not been on a train that was on time this year. Besides they usually cancelled more trains than they ran.

"They would have passed no language test that I can think of," remonstrated Henry, "except possibly our own."

"Well there you are," beamed Quentin. "Make it our own!" His hands assumed enthusiastic proportions. "Ninety seven per cent pass rate! Who knows? We could even achieve...!"

"Don't you think it's a little dishonest, Quentin?"

"They're here for a cultural and learning experience," insisted Quentin.

At ONTI? Cultural? He looked at Quentin suspiciously. He must have acquired the collocation from one of those dull sporadic workshops.

Quentin was now more composed. "I think we can let your little aberration go for the time being."

Aberration? Go? What was he talking about?

"Normally this would constitute a formal reprimand but I feel we can draw a veil over it. This time...", he added ominously.

Veil? Aberration? Was he supposed to be grateful?

He gazed over at Biggles, overseer of both UNIT and ONTI, in disbelief.

But more importantly he seemed to hear the words of Bernie who had so aptly subverted the name of Narsell. It took someone from another cultural perspective to show them the stunningly obvious.

"I think perhaps not," replied Henry.

"Perhaps not, what?" echoed Biggles.

"Not a veil."

## Icarus In Reverse

Biggles was not following him. Shouldn't it have been 'no avail'?

"I don't want a veil. I'm not a bloody bride!"

"Henry!" Biggles appeared hurt.

"You know what?" said Henry. "I think I'd rather leave."

Biggles shrank back in his chair. Disbelief and incredulity spread across his face as if a Zeppelin had floated past Sid Nuttall's plate glass windows.

"Steady on, old boy!"

Steady on, nothing!

"I think I'd like to leave," insisted Henry.

Quentin helped himself to a glass of water in an attempt to compose himself.

"Well, there's your notice for a start, isn't there? Two months?"

"No," persisted Henry, "I think I'd like to leave this week. Will Friday do you?"

Biggles crouched back further in his chair. He looked withered, deflated.

But Henry was back inside his greenhouse, beaming at the obdurate orchid that only this day had suddenly and spectacularly flowered. And next to him was the smiling face of Bernie who had so deftly renamed Biggles.

"Kop kun krap," said Henry, voicing the only Thai words he knew.

"Pardon!" exclaimed an even more mystified Biggles.

*Dominic O'Sullivan*

# Nocturne

I'm lying now in darkness. Something woke me up, scuttling below the open window. Sash windows, of course, left open in equal measure at top and bottom allowing air to circulate.

It's still warm and my eyes avoid the illuminated clock from its vantage point on the chest of drawers. If I see the time I will start to think; mind cogs whirring endlessly away. And I don't want to think. Want to sleep, to melt away back into the void.

And now as I'm thinking this I go back to that particular day which will never recede, or disappear.

I distract myself with what might have been under the window. Next door's cat most probably; a nocturnal, serial killer with its own agenda of carnage. Or an owl possibly, though it's not the time. Equinox, is the time to hear them – male and females in night-time conversations.

I used to like to listen to them with Jean. To the owl that favoured the lime tree in the adjoining garden. In July the heady scent would filter into the bedroom and from the delicate flowers you could make a kind of tea.

And now she floats back into the room – from the association of the owl.

It was a spring day when they told me. Came to see me at the office. I was standing on a pair of steps, fixing a light-bulb, throwing light onto the confines of work.

## Icarus In Reverse

I'd often contemplated escape – thought about a change of scene. When those rare interviews came they were always polite and cordial but the acceptances never arrived. Perhaps it was the digits that went to make up my age. Not so old but not so young. In a kind of limbo perhaps.

So I was up the ladder, quite literally! It was only when I came down I noticed how young they were. One had Community something written on his back. Ah well.

They asked me my name. Asked if Jean was my partner.

Wife actually, I said. They didn't smile back. Engrossed in the solemnity of the moment. Gravity as opposed to levity.

Jean was shopping, they said. Collapsed suddenly. Taken to A&E. I thought for a moment it was another kind of shop. Attempts to revive her...

I looked at the pair of steps and folded them away. They gave me a lift in a car with child-locks. Children leading children.

There were contents of course I could take home. A purse; some other things. Jean's life contained in a small dark handbag. Door keys; a stick of eau-de-cologne. She would rub it on whenever she had a headache.

And later on, when I was alone too, when everyone had gone, I took the stick and rolled it across my forehead. And as I did so, I wondered, for a moment, if there was a part of her there, a fragment of her left, as I rubbed it gently, slowly, above my eyes – endlessly rolling.

# In Passing

"Thunder-bugs," said the woman approaching me on the path.

I paused for a moment and smiled. Had she said 'Thunder-bugs'?

"I saw you itching," she explained, "seeking the cause of your irritation."

There was something theatrical in her voice. I gazed at my bare, slightly bronzed arms. Three or four dark flecks suddenly wiggled.

"They're the sign of a weather change, you know. Storm most likely. Most people are unaware."

And so was I.

"They can make your hair itch," she continued.

I brushed them away from my arms, my face.

"They're actually a kind of scorpion. If you look, you'll notice its tail waggles."

I must have appeared alarmed.

"Completely harmless, of course. As are the real things very often. Scorpions that is, provided you leave them alone."

Two dark shapes suddenly hurled themselves between us. I saw that she was carrying a pair of dog leads in her left hand.

"Turd-droppers," she said dismissively. "That's what Betjeman called them. And I have a feeling he was right."

I was confused. Dog owners were normally so proud of their charges, almost to the point of...

"I'll have to sit down a moment."

She pointed breathlessly at the conveniently located seat.

"They're not yours, then?" I enquired.

She looked at me startled.

"Oh, heavens, yes. You didn't think I was one of those professional dog-walkers, did you? Did it for a living?"

"Well, I..."

"No, no. They're very much mine, or should I say Arthur's?"

Arthur?

"My husband," she continued. "He suddenly went all doggy in his early fifties."

"Oh."

"Personally, I've never been very keen on animals, at least not the ones that trek around with humans. Poor things! They probably don't know what they are. A sort of canine schizophrenia."

I sat mesmerised on the bench overlooking the sea. I had never heard a dog owner speak so...

"In my opinion, animals should be made to work. It's better for them. Gives them a purpose in life."

I was expecting a lurch onto the unemployed, many of whom had gravitated towards seaside towns.

"It's all provided for. I mean, look at cats. Would you entertain someone in your home that didn't do a scrap of work all day, lounged around in fact, waiting to be fed?"

It was not a question that required an answer and she sallied forth again.

"And dogs are even worse! At least cats show a bit of initiative, a bit of independence; a talent for self-amusement."

I briefly pictured murder in the garden. A frog, a lizard or a butterfly...

"But dogs! Constantly seeking attention, approbation and..."

There was a pause.

"What about you?" she suddenly asked, remembering that she had a listener.

"I...I'm not a pet owner," I replied. "I don't have the time."

"Very wise. Your life's not your own."

"I suppose not."

"The odd thing was that as soon as Arthur got the dogs, he seemed to go off sex."

She pronounced 'off' as 'orf'. It was getting worse. I shifted my feet uneasily in my sandals and thought about leaving. Four dark flecks wiggled above my ankles.

"He was too busy. And too tired, I suppose. Always walking the damn things. The first two dogs were those ugly boxers, Aggy and Anka. Bitches. Whenever I was amorous with Arthur in the kitchen, Aggy, or it could have been the other one, used to barge between us. Quite literally! It was rather a heavy dog; physically strong too. I was nearly knocked off my perch several times. From time to time I used to poke Anka on the nose, or it could have been the other one, and Arthur would look at me, draw himself up, all aggrieved and say 'Was that really necessary?' As if I had done it to *him!* Fortunately Aggy was run over by Mr Donaldson reversing into his drive one September morning and I felt a burden lifted. I used to give Mr Donaldson courgettes from the garden thereafter as a token of my appreciation. And then when the other one died, Arthur got these two. Always walking them, he was. And then one day, all of a sudden, his old ticker packed up on Hanwold Heath. A policeman came to tell me along with the two dogs. They were pulling him this way and then that..."

"I'm sorry," I said, interrupting, though she didn't appear to hear.

"And so he left me with..."

She pointed at the two dark shapes, pink tongues violently wagging.

"What kind are they?" I asked.

"Some kind of crossbreed. I never bothered to find out. I was still annoyed about the boxers! Eight years it was! I suppose it could have been worse. Emily Tomlinson had a Chihuahua that went beyond sixteen."

She mentioned Emily as if I knew her.

"Well I must..." I began, attempting to stand up.

There was cramp suddenly in my left leg, something I hadn't had since opening the batting for my local cricket club.

"He made me promise not to give them away. That was after he had his first scare. 'Don't pass 'em on, El...'"

L? Laura perhaps? Or Lucy? The first suggestion of a name. Normally it came at the beginning of an encounter but in this case Arthur and the interrupted marital life preceded. Leone? Lucy? She looked more like a Leonora.

"So I haven't, of course," she continued. "Haven't handed over the reins."

"It's difficult," I said and was surprised at my own voice, my feeble response. What did *I* know?

"Yes," she said.

It was then that I noticed the vividness of her blue eyes, her pear-like head tilted like a coy schoolgirl's. The dogs bounded back together, sensing the loss of their owner. A trail of saliva plopped onto the sandy path.

"Well I must be off," she said. "Another twenty minutes at least."

She made it sound measured, like a timetable. An unfulfilled chore.

I saw her from the cliff path gently descend onto the beach. The dogs were charging ahead, annoying walkers, obliterating a last sandcastle.

Something tickled in my ear. It was another thunder-bug.

*Dominic O'Sullivan*

# Listening

When Sybil came to stay she said what no one else had quite managed to put into words. Oh of course they had made various pained expressions in the past and sometimes rolled their eyes. But they'd never said it directly. Not really.

"He talks too much," she said at tea-time.

Hazel glanced up from her bourbon biscuit. "Perhaps a little," she conceded.

"No, no." insisted Sybil. "Too much. Maybe you're not aware but..."

Hazel picked up a second biscuit. "It's because he's nervous probably."

"I don't think there's a *shred* of nerves," retorted Sybil. "It's just typical male know-all!"

Her words resonated against the pale blue china, as if she had said more than she should. Hazel gathered up the plates, temporarily avoiding eye contact with Sybil.

"It's not that he's *not* welcoming," her guest added, feeling obliged now to temper criticism with faint praise. "It's just..."

A little tiring, Hazel thought. She could happily finish the sentence for her, only not say it. Not allowed. There was the loyalty factor, of course. Loyalty to Dennis, who, once ensconced in his appropriately rigid high-backed chair, sallied forth like a tribal elder or minor politician and to whose listener the right of reply was seldom acknowledged or granted. Dennis spoke but hardly ever listened. It was as if the two were mutually exclusive; any responses from his unfortunate partner would inconveniently deflect him from his pre-ordained path. It also gave credence to the old Indian adage that the tongue indeed makes the ear deaf.

Beneath Sybil's observation lay a deeper criticism, perhaps as to a choice of spouse acquired somewhat later in life and a product of several church council meetings. Hazel had possibly chosen rashly, poorly and unwisely. Conscious of Sybil's feelings, she sat uncomfortably now in the sitting room that evening, after the washing up, while Dennis discussed and they sat listening.

He was putting the economy to rights, as he so often did, and was not to be deflected by Sybil and her logic.

"No." He tapped his pipe on the edge of the armchair, a habit which annoyed Hazel at the best of times. "There's no such thing as mental illness. It's just an invention! A name! It's sheer laziness; an unwillingness to work! To really do something! To get off their fat proverbial backsides and actually do something!"

"But, dear, what about...?" ventured Hazel.

"No matter what you say, work is a structure. It gives a sense of purpose, of value. It's just that they think it's *beneath* them and so they retreat into their shadows of alcoholism, of drugs and inertia. And the reason for this is they have no backbone! They're frightened to take responsibility!"

You make it all sound so simple, thought Sybil. 'Work sets you free', perhaps. She doubted whether Dennis would get the allusion but he might.

"Maybe," suggested Hazel, "we could all go for a little walk. It's a glorious evening."

Dennis failed to respond or even to look at the origin of the voice. Hazel glanced at Sybil for support but already she had been swept into the next line of argument which she, Hazel, had predicted.

"The Welfare State," Dennis intoned. "The culture of dependency..."

Hazel groaned inwardly. This was a long one with many side-shoots. It always was. She gazed around the room and beyond the window, where groups of birds had assembled on the lawn. They bounced around as if on springs.

"The culture of dependency. How wise America was not to choose that particular path, although with that new chap at the helm it looks like they very well might. And where would that get them? In the same mess that we're in over here with people popping across for operations, plastic surgery and the like! The health tourists!"

Hazel wanted Sybil to look away, to see what she could see bobbing up and down on the neatly cut lawn. A thrush! Something that had been missing from the garden for some while but was now making a trilling and triumphant return. It seemed larger than usual, as if it had increased during its absence. Possibly a mistle thrush. And then from time to time, in the early evening, sweeping in like some comic assassin to polish off the flying ants departing from the nest, was that bright, yellow green and red bird, the yaffle, the oddly laughing woodpecker.

This was the world outside, a world free of polemic that breathed and moved. A world with its intricate chain of dependencies, its predators.

But Sybil had been sucked in foolishly as an unwilling participant, her bristling, bridling body language having to cope with the barbs of Dennis, the gibes and snide comments; a verbal tennis match whose only function was to secure victory for the incumbent.

Sybil was riled now. Really riled. She could see. She was standing up and shouting at him but Dennis sat there implacable and unruffled, enjoying the situation, a curved finger of explanation ready to pick holes in Sybil's nebulous argument.

What did it matter anyway? His opinions were so absurd, not to mention ridiculous, that it was pointless dwelling on

## Icarus In Reverse

them. Yet Sybil had walked headlong into Dennis's polemical trap and it would be up to *him* when Sybil would be released.

Unable to stand it any longer and frustrated by her friend's lack of eye contact, she opened the French windows that gave out onto the garden. Neither of them noticed her leave, engrossed in their strategic game of verbal chess.

It was cooler outside now as the westerly evening sun was unable to radiate here through panes of glass. Instead it cast shadows onto peonies and rose-bushes. It dappled the clumps of montbretia that clustered round the shallow pond. At times smooth newts came to the surface for air or males stalked their chosen females attentively. Lucky them, she thought. At least they didn't have to cope with a surfeit of words, of argumentative and ill-tempered monologues that were dressed up as conversation.

She flicked a stone into the pool and saw it hesitate for the briefest of seconds before tumbling sideways into a clump of weed. A camouflaged leg appeared; a few bubbles blew towards the surface.

Animated cries were wafting now from the sitting room. She could hear Dennis working up to his loftier pitch, the one that was not far from securing victory, punctuated only by Sybil's feeble and flustered protests. Hazel sat on the bench for some while, watching the sun gradually disappear behind the steep, tree-lined hills, but Sybil did not re-emerge.

It was nearly ten o'clock when she turned the stiff handle of the French window to see the outline of Dennis avidly watching the news. Normally he would make a pronouncement, a recommendation that the local council or government needed shooting but this time he was silent.

"Good night, dear," she called out. There was no reply. Perhaps he had not heard her come in.

Upstairs the guest's bedroom door was slightly ajar. As she glanced inside she could see Sybil framed between the bed and wardrobe, hands working quickly and feverishly. She was piling clothes into a suitcase.

"Sybil?" She pushed open the door.

"It's okay," came the uneven reply. "I've ordered a taxi!"

"A taxi! At this time of night! But why?"

"I wouldn't be able to sleep," she protested. "Not after..." She snapped the clips of the case to.

"I was hoping to catch your eye. Hoping that you'd come outside."

"I *couldn't* let it go," Sybil trembled. "Not after what *he* was saying!"

"I take no notice," soothed Hazel. "I have to. You mustn't..."

She saw Sybil's hands were shaking as she pressed against the sides of the suitcase.

"If you have to go, could you not see your way to leaving early in the morning?"

"Out of the question," came the reply. "Thank you, Hazel. Thank you for everything but I just need to be back at home now. In my own space!"

The taxi arrived during Question Time, when Dennis would usually address various snorts and remarks towards the telly. Hazel wondered about telling him that Sybil was about to leave but thought better of it. She would explain everything in the morning when the impact would be greater.

She saw the taxi wobble slowly over the speed hump at the end of the close and then turn left at the corner. The telly flickered manically, jaggedly in the darkened sitting room.

Once upstairs she silently undressed for bed. At one o'clock she awoke and went to replenish her night time glass of water. The space next to her was still vacant. From time to time he stayed up to watch a late night film and the following morning would be taken up with a breakdown of the plot.

She went into the sitting room, saw the cushion lying on the floor, saw him sitting in the upright chair, head flung

*Icarus In Reverse*

backwards, mouth open. Pressing the remote control that had fallen onto the carpet, she turned off the yapping telly.

There was silence – a complete and sudden burst of silence.

She smiled.

## The Uncertainties of Verbs

It was the supermarket's fault, Stanley thought, as he watched the indignant Pru scurrying down the drive. Their fault as well as that unfortunate bottle of Casco de Nasco. He had tried to follow her, persuade her, but her rapid arm movements were assuming dangerous proportions. Stanley went back in and closed the front door, listening to the ensuing silence of the house. Silence.

Ashley had been ominously cheerful that day. He had arrived in a blanket of soft drizzle, enough to dampen anyone's mood, and yet there was something in his step when he crossed the threshold that betokened energy, alertness even.

"How are you, Ashley?" he enquired.

Ashley gaped back as if startled by the question. "Fine, Mr Melton. And you?"

"Yes, very good, thank you."

They perched at their usual table flanked by the regular accoutrements. There was the pocket dictionary, the larger one and the oddly-coloured blue and orange grammar book.

"Buenos dias!" said Stanley lapsing into Spanish.

"Oh yes," responded Ashley. "Bwenosh deeash."

Stanley briefly adjusted his spectacles. Pronunciation had never been Ashley's strong point. It was sometimes questionable even in English. However his reply was better articulated this time.

"Que tal?" continued Stanley, optimistically.

"Kittal?" replied Ashley without conviction.

"Si, si. Que tal?"

"Que se yo!" responded Ashley.

Stanley was momentarily perplexed. The pronunciation was perfect although it was a brilliant non-sequitur. He had wondered whether it was wise to have introduced Ashley to the 'what do *I* know?' refrain. It seemed it could be used willy-nilly, at random, and to cover a multitude of misunderstandings.

"Muy bien," said Stanley and resorted to his coloured pencils.

He had taught Ashley for nearly two years, though regrettably after every holiday, Ashley seemed to totter alarmingly backwards, almost to a state of linguistic amnesia. Old ground had to be trodden again before they could advance gingerly onto a lawn of new discoveries.

"Donde es la senora Meltona?" enquired Ashley.

This was a further surprise. An unsolicited question and a heady moment of initiative!

"En el supermercado," replied Stanley. "Como siempre."

Had he said it with a 'd' or a 't'? If it was a 't', then he was in danger of mixing it up with Italian, something which used to happen when he became knackered during the evening classes.

"Donde *esta*?" corrected Stanley. "It's a temporary state."

Ashley gazed back at him blankly.

Why did Spanish have to have two words for the verb 'to be', two forms, when Ashley could barely manage one? But then given Pru's increasing predilection for visiting the out of town supermarket, one that made good use of her still free bus pass, then perhaps the permanent quality of the Spanish verb *was* more appropriate. There was also no need to add to the surname and create a senora Meltona. It was not Russian after all. But wisely Stanley considered it was better to pursue one avenue of correction at a time.

"Donde *esta* la senora?" he said to Ashley, who was looking at a wood pigeon through the living room window.

"En la cava," replied Ashley oddly.

Stanley reached for the guided security of the grammar book. Now was a good moment to reprise those basic verbs.

"What about a tea, Ashley?" he suddenly asked a while later. It was good to break up the routine, to relax a little.

"Muy gracias," answered Ashley.

He stood up and walked over to the sitting room window while Stanley fiddled about with the tea-making. Ashley was growing taller he noticed, blotting out the light from the window. Now that they had moved away from the uncertainties of verbs, Ashley resumed his cheerfulness.

"Have you had some good news, Ashley?" Stanley enquired as he brought in the tea tray. There was a pink cake with butter icing.

"Good news, Mr Melton?"

"Exams or something?"

No. It was only March. It couldn't be.

"No, no, it's me birthday. It means I'm legal."

Oh, thought Stanley, regretting the lack of light in the living room. Legal for what? For some reason he had a bizarre image of Ashley fornicating on a milk-float – his dad had once been their milkman – and quickly dismissed it. Nevertheless, it returned as Stanley dug a spoon into the sugar bowl. It was odd to think of one's pupils as having sex lives.

"Well, then, if you're legal, this calls for a celebration."

Stanley went over to the sideboard and opened the bottom drawer.

"A glass of sherry, perhaps?"

"I've never 'ad sherry," Ashley replied.

"It's Spanish, actually," smiled Stanley, "so it's quite appropriate."

"What's sherry in Spanish?" asked Ashley.

## Icarus In Reverse

As he poured the pale gleaming brown liquid into two crystal glasses Stanley's mind suddenly went blank. Blanker than it did at the end of the evening classes which he had taught at the Institute and where Cynthia Fairweather, who had a notable crush on him, had attended Beginners' for over four years. Perhaps this would be the same with Ashley, he thought, and momentarily shivered.

"Er, sherry is sherry," stumbled Stanley.

It was still not quite right. He was distracted by the momentousness of the occasion – Ashley's big day.

"Oh well," said Ashley. "That's easy, then." He took a large gulp of the pale liquid. "You know, Mr Melton, it's them big words that are easy in Spanish. You know, investigation, constipation, information. And if you lisp 'em, they're almost the same."

Stanley stared across at Ashley. The sherry was having a surprising effect. It was not often that Ashley was given to independent thought.

"Hot in here," said Ashley, running a finger round his T-shirt collar. His cheeks were suddenly very red.

"I'll turn the heating down in a moment," offered Stanley.

He liked to have the house warm for Pru, especially when she returned from those shopping trips. She always felt the cold.

"You said, Ashley, about being legal. Legal for what?"

Almost immediately he regretted the question. He could hear the word 'shagging' blowing in the tunnel of reply and once again saw Ashley ensconced on a milk float.

"Voting," announced Ashley with solemnity. "Voting."

He said it with an almost northern twang and then Stanley remembered that his mum came from Ramsbottom.

"Are you sure, Ashley?" he said. "I thought it was eighteen."

Perhaps he was now. He'd been teaching him for so long; the well-trodden Beginners' path where footsteps had worn away the flagstones.

"Is it?" said Ashley. "Are you sure?"

"Are you eighteen, then?"

Ashley's face fell. "I thought it were sixteen."

He drained the rest of his sherry glass.

"There was some talk, you know, about reducing the voting age," offered Stanley consolingly.

"I were looking forward to it, Mr Melton."

Perhaps this had explained his exuberance, his new initiative, his sudden resourcefulness, charged with a heady sense of responsibility. The nation suddenly in people like Ashley's hands. Maybe not, he thought as he refilled the empty glass.

"I'll just turn the heating down," he said, remembering.

As he stepped into the hallway there was a sudden beeping which he realised was the new phone.

"I'll just be a moment, Ashley."

He picked up the receiver wondering if it was the questionnaire lady who mysteriously rang from India. Instead he could hear the husky tones of Pru.

"I'm inside Dudgeon's," she breathed. "They've got a phone you can use by the vegetable counter."

"I see," responded Stanley. "Is everything okay?"

"Of course it is," said Pru, resenting the question. "No, they've got a phone here and it's very convenient. I thought I'd take advantage of it."

On that basis Pru could ring him from unlimited locations, or every time there was a suitably vacant phone.

"I've got Ashley with me," he replied, hoping that it would shorten the conversation.

"Yes I know you have. I'm just ringing to see if we have any yoghurts. There's a special offer on. Could you take a look in the fridge, dear?"

## Icarus In Reverse

Obligingly Stanley laid down the receiver and trotted into the kitchen. The brightly lit up refrigerator revealed a solitary pot of fromage frais.

"We've got none," he answered.

"Well it's good that I rang, then. That's the beauty of these phones. Now what flavours should I get?"

"Lemon...er, hazelnut, and the blackcurrant is particularly fine. Are they the yoghurts from Yorkshire?"

"I don't know, dear. I think it said 'Skipton'. I'll just take a look."

"Er, Pru..."

He heard the clunk as the receiver dangled, the far away noise of distant shoppers, patrolling trolleys and a musical announcement. After about three minutes Pru returned.

"I've just put some more money in," she announced. "Raspberry, pear and vanilla."

"I think raspberry and vanilla."

"Pear and vanilla?"

"No, raspberry."

"The pear comes with the vanilla. It's pear *and* vanilla."

The combination seemed less appetising.

"Just the raspberry, dear."

"All right. And what about some tinned soups? They're on offer, too."

"All right, Ashley?" Stanley called out to him.

From the living room came a kind of 'oink'.

"Just a minute," said Pru.

"Oh no!" protested Stanley, but the phone clunked again and dangled, pirouetting to a staff announcement for Mr Barclay.

After an interminable interlude in which three more announcements were delivered, Pru returned.

"Three bean spicy, tomato and Worcester sauce, cannelloni and West Country vegetable."

The descriptions were getting longer.

"But there can't be a cannelloni soup," argued Stanley. "It's pasta, isn't it?"

"Just a moment."

Pru was off again.

"All right, Ashley? Just talking to Pru."

This time there was a grunt followed by a strange swishing sound.

"It's minestrone, dear."

"I *must* go, dear. I've got Ashley."

"You haven't said which soup!"

"All four. The cannelloni and the oxtail."

"There was no oxtail, dear!"

"Yes there was. You said West Country oxtail."

Why the West Country should have a special claim to oxtail was beyond him.

"I'll go and check."

Stanley let out a strangulated cry of despair.

"I'm fine," replied Ashley from the living room.

"Very good," replied Stanley, listening intently for Pru. In the background he could hear a mixture of new sounds.

"I'll go and have a look for you, dear," said a voice – not Pru's – but which echoed her words to Stanley.

There was a sputtering at the other end.

"I've just put in fifty pee," said Pru. "It'll be all right for a while."

Stanley stood glued to the phone, mopping his brow, thinking about Spanish irregular verbs. They were always the most common ones, he decided. The ones you needed most. It was very unfair on the learners.

"No oxtail," said Pru, vindicated after another lengthy wait. "West Country Vegetable."

"All three! All four! As many as you like! Now I *must* go, dear!"

"Well there's no need to be irritable, Stanley! Sally's gone to a lot of trouble."

## Icarus In Reverse

"Sally?"

"Yes."

"Well thank you very much, dear."

He put the phone down before Pru could proceed further and stepped apologetically into the living room.

He was not prepared for the sight that greeted him. He blinked and looked again. A near naked Ashley was draining off the final drops of Casco de Nasco.

"Ashley! What on earth!"

"I hope you don't mind."

"Ashley!"

"It got so hot in here and I seemed to come out in one of those flushes. Me mam usually gets them during Come Dancing or the repeats of Jason King."

"But she doesn't disrobe in the sitting room, surely?"

"No, no." Ashley giggled suddenly.

It was then that Stanley realised his student was completely and hopelessly drunk.

"Ah could get a likin' fer this," said Ashley, pointing to the empty bottle and sounding northern again.

"Very likely."

"And after that disappointment."

"What disappointment?"

"Well, ah thought ah could vote."

He drew the last word out into two syllables.

"But that's no reason for intoxication of this kind!"

At that moment he realised that all under-age binge drinkers that thronged the market squares on Friday evenings were in fact disenfranchised voters.

"El sherry, muy bien. Me gusta muchissimo!"

Ashley was truly drunk. He now seemed to be speaking only in Spanish.

"Ashley, put some clothes on!"

"Hola. Encantado. No soy constipado."

"Estoy," corrected Stanley. "Now, *please*, Ashley!"

"Hace calor. Hace calor," protested Ashley, waving an imaginary fan.

Stanley was astonished. Ashley had never used these words before.

"Ah yes. Of course. I'll just go and turn it down. Now meantime, could you pop back into some clothes for me?"

"Claro," burped Ashley. "Claro que si."

If only he had supplied small glasses of Casco de Nasco to his evening classes, he ruminated. The end of term results might have been so different.

He went out into the hallway to turn the heating down, leaving Ashley in search of a pale grey sock. The door to the small cupboard under the stairs obstinately snagged against the carpet. Stanley tried again, pulling it with all his might, while Ashley gave a strange grunt from the living room. Stanley tugged again but this time the door came to meet him. He fell into it, tumbled towards the switches and controls...

When Pru inserted her key into the lock, leaving the taxi that had accommodated her shopping to swivel back down the drive, she found a pale shape groping on the other side of the door.

As she stepped into the hallway the shape, wearing only a pair of tropical boxer shorts, ran past her.

"Hace calor! Hace calor!" the shape repeated. Then, "Buenos dias, Mrs Mutton!"

"Ashley!"

She saw him skipping haphazardly down the drive singing something that sounded like 'Viva Espana'. Getting up from the hallway, with a strange red swelling on his forehead, was Stanley.

"Pru!" he exclaimed. "That was quick!"

"I got a taxi," she said, offering a face like thunder.

"Ah," acknowledged Stanley.

"If *that's* what you get up to when I'm down at the supermarket...!"

## Icarus In Reverse

"Up to? Up to what? What do you mean?"

"I've just seen Ashley," she said, trying to sound calm. "He was both naked and indecent!"

"But he..."

"If that's your aim to ply young men with drink and then seduce them while I'm down at Dudgeon's, then I wish to have nothing more to..."

"But he said he was legal! And then I told him..."

"Oh! Oh! So that makes it all right, does it? The fact that he's legal? And shouldn't you have told me earlier that you liked young boys in boxer shorts?"

"But I don't!" protested Stanley. "Besides, it was all *your* fault!"

"My fault! My fault!" raged Pru. "How dare you, Stanley Melton! How dare you! How dare you suggest that it is *I* who have turned you into a homosexual!"

"But if you hadn't rung up, dear..."

"I suppose you were already in the middle of something! No wonder you were so irritable when I was sorting out the soups. Coitus interruptus, I suppose!"

Stanley was about to point out that it was technically incorrect, that nothing really *had* taken place, when a pot of vanilla yoghurt flew past his ear. This was followed by a few other unidentifiable flavours. Stanley fled back into the kitchen. The soup tins would be next and they were far more lethal. Besides, he already had a large bump on his head from the stairway cupboard.

There was a brief silence. Then the front door banged to. He ran out into the hall, remonstrating. Pru was scurrying frantically down the drive, discarded shopping lying at the bottom of the stairs. He tried to follow her but her rapid arm movements were assuming ominous proportions.

He closed the door after her and listened to the eerie silence of the house.

And then he thought of Ashley.